Charlotte Cole grew ⎯⎯⎯⎯⎯⎯⎯⎯⎯⎯
London to take a degree in English ⎯⎯
Sunrise to Sunset: An Anthology of Summer Reading (The
Women's Press, 1997), *Between You and Me: Real-life
Diaries and Letters by Women Writers* (Livewire, 1998), and
co-edited (with Helen Windrath), *The Female Odyssey:
Visions for the 21st Century* (The Women's Press, 1999).
She is an editor at The Women's Press.

Also edited by Charlotte Cole from The Women's Press:

Sunrise to Sunset: An Anthology of Summer Reading (1997)
Between You and Me: Real-life Diaries and Letters by Women Writers (Livewire Books for young women, 1998)
The Female Odyssey: Visions for the 21st Century (1999)

first frost

An Anthology of Winter Reading

CHARLOTTE COLE, EDITOR

First published by The Women's Press Ltd 1998
A member of the Namara Group
34 Great Sutton Street, London EC1V 0DX

Collection copyright © The Women's Press, 1998

The copyright in each of the pieces in this collection remains with the original copyright holder.

The right of the contributors to be identified as the joint authors of this work has been asserted by them in accordance with the Copyright, Designs and Patents Act 1988.

British Library Cataloguing-in-Publication Data
A catalogue record for this book is available from the British Library.

ISBN 0 7043 4609 5

Typeset in Goudy Old Style 10.5/13pt by FSH Ltd, London
Printed and bound in Great Britain by Cox & Wyman Ltd,
Reading, Berkshire

contents

Introduction		1
Ice	Toni Cade Bambara	3
Fish	Michèle Roberts	12
The Company of Wolves	Angela Carter	19
Cap O'Rushes	A.L. Kennedy	30
Hack Wednesday	Margaret Atwood	44
Ice Castle	Becky Birtha	66
The Wedding Dress	Mary Flanagan	96
Solo	Lucy Jane Bledsoe	122
Old Ones Become Birds	Patricia Grace	132
Love Poem	Githa Hariharan	136
Chemistry	Carol Shields	145
The World With Love	Ali Smith	163
The River and the		
Red Spring Moon	Patricia Duncker	170
Chipmunk	Jane Rogers	175
Girls on Ice	Helen Dunmore	184
Contributors' Notes		191
Permissions		197

INTRODUCTION

The best place to read *First Frost* is curled up in an armchair by the fireplace. These stories should be read under a thick duvet in bed, looking out on to a snow-bright winter's night; or all wrapped up on a park bench, with the fresh wind whipping at your ears. In compiling *First Frost* I looked for stories that would melt your emotions and truly warm your heart.

The dangers of the colder months are explored in Toni Cade Bambara's 'Ice', where only the neighbourhood children notice the suffering of creatures as small as puppies. In 'Girls on Ice', Ulli and Edith walk out on an ice-covered sea, not counting on another heavy fall of snow. And in Angela Carter's classic tale, 'The Company of Wolves', we find a landscape where wolves are never far from your door.

Winter is always a time that stirs the memory. In Carol Shields' 'Chemistry', a woman reflects back to the friendships gained and lost in an evening recorder class over two decades before. 'Solo' follows a woman taking a lone cross-country skiing trip, in the remembrance of her friend Elizabeth, who died in an avalanche on a similar trek; and 'The World With Love' shows how a chance encounter reminds Sam of her teenage passion for French – and of her first love.

Love appears again in 'Chipmunk', as a couple take a belated honeymoon and wonder if they've left it too late to find romance; and 'Ice Castle', where Maurie experiences a painful unrequited love for a woman unsuitable in so many ways. 'The Wedding Dress' has Nora discovering that a little shrewdness can go a long way to set a marriage on the right tracks. And meanwhile Neeta, in Githa Hariharan's 'Love Poem', learns a little more about love than she'd like!

A woman leaves her 'goblin' husband and sons and strikes out for permanent independence in A.L. Kennedy's 'Cap O'Rushes'; while in 'Fish' a young girl escapes with her imaginary dog Jeremy just for a while, until her parents calm down and her home is welcoming once more. In 'The River and the Red Spring Moon', a woman has to cope on her own after the death of her second husband by drowning – but she might be finding it easier than you'd think…

The first frosts of autumn, inevitably, bring thoughts about the passing of time. And Margaret Atwood's examination of this, in 'Hack Wednesday', is impeccable as – with Christmas and New Year fast approaching – Marcia worries about her job, her husband and the world. But in 'Old Ones Become Birds', set at a Maori meeting, the old people find their own way of living.

The short story can be a slice of life or a tale of generations, but like the myriad patterns of a snowflake, and the infinite variations of a life, each story is unique.

Charlotte Cole

ice

TONI CADE BAMBARA

None of the grown-ups can look us kids in the face because of the puppies. They must have been squealing in the cold, and Lady, the mama dog, probably raced from door to door scratching and howling trying to get somebody's attention. It must have been awful for her. The grown-ups can't say they weren't around and didn't know the pups were freezing, because every single one of them was at home all day long. Folks who work at the post office work nights. Folks who work at the hospital are still out on strike. Folks who work at the bottling plant were laid off till further notice. And folks who work in the city were excused from their jobs because the highways aren't clear yet.

Seems to me the old men who live on the corner with the meanest dog in the world could have taken the puppies in, put them in a box with an old sock or two, and set them in the basement away from Mean Dog. And the crazy old lady who lives at the other end of the block could have called them in. They would have come. Puppies don't have any better sense than to come to a crazy old calling lady. Somebody should have helped Lady, for there's just so much a mama can do. At least that's what my mama is always saying when she throws down the dish towel and stomps off to her studio back of the house.

We kids left for school this morning muffled to our eyes in pulled-up collars and yanked-down caps and scarves wrapped round and round like bandits. We stumbled along to the bus in layers and layers of clothing, shouting to Lady to get her pups out of the street. Little Marcy was shooing them away from Mean Dog's yard because Mean Dog is likely to break his chain and attack anything and everything in sight. Last month, for example, when Lady's litter was barely walking, he broke loose and got hold of three pups. Our parents kept calling us in. The weatherman had said a storm was coming up fast. But we were busy beating Mean Dog with our book satchels and lunch buckets to make him let go of the puppies. It was like a shark movie when Mean Dog got hold of the runt and that furry little head started disappearing into that huge mouth. But then Tommy Jeeter came by on his skate board, and that was the perfect thing to go upside that mean dog's head with. He kept twisting around growling and snapping at us, but we kept shoving that skate board at him. Tommy Jeeter grabbed one of the pups and I grabbed the other. And for one wonderful moment, Mean Dog dropped the runt and backed off and Marcy almost got it. But then his huge white paw came down on the poor thing like a stone. And it got mashed so hard into the ground, you couldn't tell mud from pup from grass.

So Marcy was shooing the puppies away from Mean Dog's yard, and Marcy's mother kept hollering for her to get on the school bus with the rest of us stumbling aboard in our fat clothes like helpless astronauts. We were mumbling about the wonderful thank-you cards we would send the mayor for sending an emergency school bus and messing up our holiday. And then we were banging on the windows, trying to tell anybody who could hear us to get Lady and her puppies out of the cold.

Aunt Myrtle was in the driveway pouring steaming water on her car door, trying to get the lock to unfreeze. But when she saw that the key would still not turn, she just dropped the kettle right there in the driveway and scooted back into the house. It was that cold. My mama was waving the bus good-bye from the warm side of the storm door, wrapped in two quilts mummy-style with my old skating cap on her head, so I doubt she could hear. My stepfather and the two other men who led the strike at the hospital were on the curb, talking, beating their gloves together, jumping up and down in their boots and explaining ways to keep warm. At our house, we'd been burning the telephone books, the Christmas tree, gift boxes, even my old dollhouse – anything that fits in the fireplace and will give heat.

Just as the school bus pulled off, it skidded on a skin of ice on the sewer grating that's home plate in nice weather. And right away all the parents huddled in doorways in bathrobes and coats and blankets started started hollering directions to the driver to cut his wheels this way and pump the pedal that way. They were making so much noise, they didn't hear us, didn't notice Lady shivering for all her fat and fur. And the puppies, scrambling out of the street finally to take shelter in Miss Norma's carport, got no attention whatsoever.

My stepdaddy built a doghouse for Lady and the pups. But they wouldn't stay put. The day after Lady had her puppies in the carport, Miss Norma packed them in a milk crate and set them out on the sidewalk like it was a case of pickup and delivery. Me and Marcy and Tommy Jeeter went round with a coffee can I grabbed before my mama could stuff her paintbrushes in it, and we collected enough for a sack of dog meal but not enough to buy a doghouse. So we asked my stepdaddy to build one. While he sawed wood and sang work songs, we cut pictures out of Ebony and Sepia. And while he nailed the house together and sang about rivers rising and floods flooding, we went through my mama's sketchbook. And while he sanded the whole thing down, he let Tommy Jeeter hold the huge basketball of tinfoil he's been building since a long-ago

5

war, a time when the government paid people to save bacon grease and newspapers and rubber bands and things. Tommy Jeeter kept rolling the crazy thing around on the rug, saying, 'And you never once sold it.' He said that about five times. You could tell that he would have sold it; Jeeter would not have spent his life strip-mining gum and candy wrappers. It was a fine dog-house when my stepdaddy finished, but the dogs hardly ever used it. Lady was always begging up and down the block at kitchen doors, and the pups were always right behind her, 'doggin her steps' as my mother would say when she means for us kids to get out of her face so she can paint in peace.

When the school bus passed Bowker Street on the way home, we knew something bad had happened, because we didn't see Kwame on his bike throwing newspapers. It is the thing to do when you get to the corner of Bowker and Third – watch Kwame straining up the hill, standing on the pedals, his head thrown back and his hood slipping off. You think that any minute his clothes will pop loose with all that effort and fly up the hill like the kites we write wishes on and release on the first day of carnival. The bus turned into our block and we saw Kwame's bike sprawled in the middle of the street. We got off that bus so fast, we didn't even fool around with last tag and 'See you later, alligator.' We flew. Kwame was in Miss Norma's yard cracking the ground with the heel of his boot, trying to make the ice give the puppies up.

There were two of them, gray and stiff and dead. Their mouths were puckered as though somebody had come along with a sewing machine and stitched their faces. It was more like they had snarled at the end, had growled and taken their anger into death with them and would come back in the next life meaner than Mean Dog to get us for not taking care. We found the other three all piled on top of each other by the mailbox, as though they'd been waiting for the mailman with the overdue packages to take them aboard or mail them to Florida so they could live. Tommy Jeeter, his hands shoved up his armsleeves, kept jiggling from one foot to the other, saying, 'Oh wow, oh wow.' He'd said, back when Lady's belly was dragging the ground and she could barely sneak up on the squirrels, that he wanted to train one of the litter as a hunting dog to present to his uncle. Sweet Pea and Brenda buried their faces in each other's furry shoulders and hugged each other's coat sleeves. Joanne just stood there watching Kwame with his pick-'n'-axe boot, cracking that same gum our teacher had tried to get her to throw away all day. Me and Marcy tried to make a fence with our legs to keep Lady away who was moaning and whining and running around in circles, trying to get to her dead puppies.

'You stupid old fool dog. Where were you when your puppies were freezing to death? Get out of here.'

'Quit yelling at her, Joanne, wasn't her fault,' Marcy tried to say. But as soon as she could get a few words out, the wind shoved them right back down her throat.

Brenda picked her face up from Sweet Pea's fur collar long enough to say, 'Suppose that was you, Joanne? You wouldn't want your mother to just walk away and leave you there.'

Joanne sucked her teeth. 'Forget you, crybaby.'

'Who you calling "crybaby"?' Sweet Pea and Brenda were ready to fight.

'Oh shut up,' Kwame said, looking around for something to put the puppies in. Marcy dumped her books right out on the ground and held her satchel open and Kwame plopped them in. I reached for a strap to help, but Marcy swung the load onto her shoulder and walked off. She looked just like the women in my mama's sketch pad, women with that same look carrying things on their back or on their heads, looking like they've just done something wonderful like dump their schoolbooks on the ground and offered their brand new book bag for toting. We all followed her to the hide-'n'-seek woods, Joanne stretching her gum in and out like she was having a very boring time.

'Hooo-hooooo.'

We were standing by the home-free-all tree watching Kwame dig a hole and none of us wanted to turn around. We knew it was the crazy old lady calling us from her house on the hill at the corner. But she kept calling, so we did turn, and right away we were sorry. There she was in her window looking like some Halloween thing, her teeth not in her mouth, her old-timey shawl looking like a huge spider web, some weird thing on her head like a bowl cover you use for keeping the onion smells out of the Jell-O. Any other time, Joanne would have said, 'I dare you to go up on to her porch and tip over her rocker.' But she didn't, went right on pulling at her gum. Any other time, Brenda and Sweet Pea would have taken off like Olympic runners, afraid the old lady might tell their grandfather she'd seen them lollygagging in the woods instead of going straight home from school. They didn't run. They kept handing Kwame sticks to dig with that kept crumbling. The ice storm had made everything brittle. Any other time I would have held my breath and prayed she wasn't calling me to pick up the pans and plates. My Aunt Myrtle always takes food to Mrs Blue because she's from 'down home', and because she knew Aunt Myrtle 'when', and because she has a 'gift', and just because. I was too cold to think of anything but how weird she looked tapping on her window with a spoon.

'Maybe she wants to give us a shovel so we can bury them,' Tommy Jeeter said. Then he grabbed Lady by the collar and took her off into the woods to find beer cans to sell to his uncle who collects them.

'Let her bring it, then,' Joanne said.

'It's cold and she's old. Why don't you go get it?'

Joanne gave Marcy a hot look. 'Forget you, Marcy.' Then she strolled off in her sheepskin coat like she was in a fashion show and we were buying.

'We gotta go,' the twins said, shivering and shaking and walking off.

'Guess God decided to take them,' Kwame said, meaning the puppies he had just buried. And it was too cold to open my mouth and say that I'd always heard that God receives, not takes. Besides, what would God want with puppies? God is not running a pound. But someone has to say some sort of words when dead bodies are put into the ground, so I shut up. After a while, Kwame nodded to Marcy and me and trotted up the block to deliver his papers. Me and Marcy stood there looking at the mound of dirt and twigs and pebbles as though a certain amount of time had to be spent standing there in silence and mourning.

'Mrs Blue is probably thinking the same thing could happen to her,' Marcy said. 'She could starve to death or freeze right there in the window and nobody would go and see about her.'

I didn't say a word. I was numb. I tried to think of something hot to warm me up while we stood at the grave. All I could think of was the fire my mama used to draw. When she was a little girl in Holly Springs, Mississippi, some do-wrong people set a torch to her daddy's farm. And there was no firehouse in the Black community then. The fire was so bad, birds fell down dead from the sky. There's a drawing in red ink and charcoal of grandma trying to beat flames from the mattress, its insides jumping all over the yard like popcorn, and the emptied-out houses and sheds and barns for miles around glowing like coals in a grate. My mama drew the trees like giants with their hair on fire racing through the fields holding their heads, then crashing down and rolling around in the cornfields burning everything up. None of this made me warm. It made my teeth chatter all the more. My bones felt like they would shatter any minute.

'Maybe we should stop by on the way home,' Marcy said. 'Poor Mrs Blue. I bet her house is like the cold box.'

And I remembered the first time I ever saw Marcy with her spatter-paint-freckled self. She was in the butcher's with her parents, reading out loud all the signs. But when the butcher opened the cold room where the meat hangs, Marcy started whimpering. There was a rabbit hanging on a hook by its tail. 'Ohhhhhhh, what have they done to the Easter bunny?'

We called her 'Cotton Tail' for a long time, until we realized she was going to ignore us until we learned to say 'Marcy.' I was going to remind her of that time, but it didn't seem right to talk about it with the puppies there under the dirt.

'I'm going to see what she wants,' Marcy finally said, and waited to see if I was going to move. I didn't. Mrs Blue is a very spooky person and her house is dark and I don't like going in there. So Marcy went off by herself.

By the time I made the rounds of the houses, reporting what had happened to the puppies, the streetlights were coming on and the moon was chasing me. For a whole hour I fussed about the puppies dying right there under everybody's noses, and Aunt Myrtle didn't tell me to hush. And my stepdaddy rubbed his forehead a lot like he had a headache. And neither of them could look me in the eye. They just said soft things, short things, like the other grown-ups on the block. 'A shame', or 'Winter's mean', or 'Poor Lady'. When I went into my mama's studio to talk some more about how it wasn't fair, five puppies freezing to death with so many grown-up people right there at home, my mama squeezed some purple paint out on her paint plate real slowlike. 'Bury them?' was all she said, and she wouldn't look me in the eye either.

I sat on my bed a long time putting together the story of the storm, how the berry bushes looked lovely at first, all silver and frosty, till the branches split and the bushes fell away. How Mrs Robinson took a spill on the ice and the ambulance driver wouldn't take her until Marcy and me ran around with that same coffee can and collected thirty-two dollars. How the second wave of snow came and piled up banks of hard ice on the curbs and against porches and steps and cars. How my dollhouse got tossed into the fire; even though I was asked and did give permission, it hurt. And how the puppies died like that. It'll be a story for my children, I was thinking, sitting on my bed, just as my stepdaddy sings about the time the river rose and his town was flooded but people rebuilt the town and everything was alright. And just as my mama draws about that fire but people rebuilt the farm and she grew up to tell us about it. But what if my kids notice there's a hole in my story, I asked myself, a hole

I will fall right through in the telling. Suppose they ask, 'But, Mommy, didn't you go and see about the old lady?' So then I'll tell them how I put my boots back on and put them silly pot-holder mittens on too to carry one of Aunt Myrtle's casseroles down to Mrs Blue. And with the moon pushing at my back, I'm thinking that maybe I'll sit with Mrs Blue a while even though she is a spooky sort of person.

From *Deep Sightings and Rescue Missions*, published by The Women's Press.

fish

MICHELE ROBERTS

There was a giant on the causeway. I watched him stride into the sky, the plumy reeds of the marsh rippling away from his right boot, and the sea, boiling up the colour of old tea, splashing back from his left. The causeway trembled as he pounded along it and the gulls wheeled off over his bristling black hair.

Once he had dwindled to human size I let go of my breath, clapped shut the back door, and returned to the queer kitchen that curved like a crescent moon. Only standing at the stove could you see both the sink and the china cupboard. Standing at one end you lost the other. The wall in the middle bulged out and hid it.

My mother fetched an egg from the black wire basket that hung in the larder, cracked it on the edge of a cup, made the yolk slip from one half of the shell to the other, let the white dangle down, plop.

Her lips changed from thin and compressed to relaxed, plump. When she moved her head a little I thought she was still trying out the effect of air moving over her bare nape. All the way back from Ipswich on the bus yesterday she had undulated her neck like a swan, one hand constantly going up to ruffle the newly short crop to search for the non-existent chignon. She'd let me finger it too, soft as swan's feathers. Now to her beauty she had added a dash of the boy, silky spikes sticking up where she'd rumpled them tracing the memory of hairpins. There were fine wrinkles about her mouth, prominent when she was cross but smoothing themselves out, as now, when she unclenched her jaw and began to smile again. The skin under her deep-set eyes was puckered, a little parched. When she remembered to she slapped beeswax on to the furniture, saddle-soap on to her boots, cream on to her face. Her cheekbones were smooth as eggs. In the summer she went brown on the first day of hot sunshine.

Today, sun and rain sparkled on the windowpane together. She was making a sauce to go with the fish and broccoli we were going to have for lunch, even though we'd only just finished breakfast. She was breathing deeply, still not quite calmed down. Sauces thickened with egg yolk, she'd explained to me many times, curdled easily if the cook was in too much of a hurry, or cross, or overheated the mixture. I watched, to see what would happen. I perched next to her, my head close to her, so that I could brush my cheek against the coarse thick cotton of her apron, snuff up her smell that was a mixture of sweat, eau-de-Cologne and warm animal.

She tilted the bowl in which the egg yolk sat, propped it on the edge of the breadboard, held the bowl steady with one hand, and whisked with the other. I held ready the little pan of melted butter, and, when she grunted, began to tip it in, drop by drop, while she beat it with her fork.

– There now, she coaxed: you're coming along really nicely, that's it, gently does it, lovely.

The egg yolk and the butter responded. She called it performing. They flowed together and thickened, and she praised them again.

13

– Quick, she said to me: now fetch the pan of fish stock and we'll drip in some of that.

I hesitated. She dropped the fork on the tabletop.

– Bloody hell. We haven't got any bloody fish because your bloody father was supposed to go and get it before breakfast and he bloody well forgot.

The egg yolk and the butter, bereft of her attention, began to separate. Smoothness and lightness broke up into little oily grains in a sort yawn, a yellow ripple of defiance.

– That's that, my mother said.

She untied the strings of her apron and threw it over the back of the kitchen chair.

– Why the hell am I thinking about lunch anyway? I must be daft.

She put out a finger and stroked the side of my neck, ear to shoulder.

– I'm no good for anything in a state like this. I'll be better off doing some writing, not faffing about down here.

She hugged me. I bit her forearm quite hard, holding the fold of skin between my teeth the way our neighbour's dog held his newspaper, pretending to worry it. She tasted of bed. She hadn't had a bath this morning. They'd overslept. That was one of the reasons my father had been so cross. Another was her having her hair cut off without asking him first.

At the first turn of the stairs she paused, to yell down to me.

– If you want to play outside don't go too far away. Stay close to the house, OK?

I pretended not to hear. She tramped on up.

Our house was right at the end of the promenade, where the pink-washed cottages stopped and the sea wall began. It used to be the coastguards' lookout. It was like a lighthouse in shape, a stumpy tower with a little rounded cap like a mushroom's. Inside it the staircase coiled round and up. On the ground floor were our curved kitchen and sitting-room, and the lean-to shed built on the side that my father used as a studio. Above this was the lodger's bedroom and the bathroom, and above that, piled on top of each other, were my parents' bedroom, my bedroom and my mother's study. At the moment, because it was the start of winter, we had no lodgers and so we were broke. That was another reason my parents had had the row last night. Shouting above the noise of the radio so that I could easily hear them next door in the kitchen where I was pretending to do some drawing.

My mother's study was the best room in the house, snug and round, with portholes, and a little white metal balcony. You had to climb up a ladder to get to it. She insisted on having it when we moved in because being right at the top of the house it was far away from my father and me. My father could paint with us listening to the radio on the other side of the open door, but my mother said she could only write when she felt completely alone. We weren't allowed in her study without her. She said we'd only mess it up. She had lovely things on her desk: little china pots, glass paperweights, a box of old nibs, a wineglass full of felt-tip pens, a red straw basket full of notebooks. It was where she went to get away from us, not only to write children's books. Sometimes on Sundays when she went up to dust I'd go with her, and she'd show me her things one by one and let me play with them.

I stood in the hall, wondering what to do. Then I saw she'd left her purse on the hall table. I decided to give her a surprise and go to fetch the fish.

I liked her purse. Worn leather sides fastened together at the top with a gilt clasp like two hands that you could click and unclick in the palm of your hand. Inside was a concertina of compartments of thin pink leather, soft as the chamois she used for cleaning the windows. Coins in one part, notes in the next, bus tickets, cinema tickets, library tickets, an old drawing of mine folded up small with dirty creases. It was a picture of her I'd done at infant school. I smoothed it out to look at it, as I always did when she gave me my pocket money. I was a good drawer, everyone said so. In the picture she had long hair, almost down to the waist. It wasn't right any more, so I tore it up and threw the pieces on the floor.

My socks were too short. The wellingtons were cold against my legs when I shoved my feet into them. I couldn't find Jeremy's lead, so I tied a piece of string on to his collar instead.

Ten steps, and I was on the beach. The sky was full of big black clouds dashing across the sun, and it was very windy. The tide was running out. I hauled Jeremy down over the shingle and on to the wet sand which was easier to walk on. There were no other dogs around so I let him off his piece of string. So far I hadn't managed to stop him wanting to fight with other dogs. He was invisible to everyone but me but other dogs always knew he was there and went for him. My father kicked them if they came too close. I wished I'd brought his stick out with me. I was thinking of the fierce Alsatian that sometimes appeared. Then I remembered the red mark my teeth had made on my mother's arm and started to whistle. I was practising in secret to surprise my father who said I was hopeless at it, girls of eight couldn't whistle and never to let him hear that screeching again.

I turned my back on our house and the causeway and the marsh beyond it and walked along close to the sea. I knew I wouldn't get lost. I would walk along as far as the fishing boats and then come back. There was no reason to hurry. On Saturday mornings the fisherman sold their catch right up until lunchtime, and it was still early. I splashed through the waves for a bit, until I got water down my boots, and then I went higher up the beach to the tideline. There was a good lot of driftwood today. I collected as much as I thought I'd be able to drag home, tied it together with my piece of string, and left it for my return journey. I was already cold, because I'd forgotten to put my windcheater on, but I was determined to stay out as long as possible. Until my mother missed me and started shouting for me, thinking I was lost.

I started to look for shells and the green bits of broken bottle, rubbed smooth by the sea, that I called jewels. I found a lot of pebbles covered with sticky black tar, a couple of dry cuttlefish, a dead seagull, several rotting fish-heads. I found just one good stone, a lump of pink quartz still glistening with sea water.

Because I was keeping my eyes down I almost bumped into the cable. It stretched across my passage, barring it. A tight twist of thick steel, two feet off the slope of the beach. One end ran straight into the sea, a little way out, and disappeared in the yellow-grey waves, and the other went tautly over the top of the hill of shingle and vanished.

My legs were tired. I sat down, propped myself against the slide of damp stones, and put my hands lightly about the cable.

It was alive. Inside the tunnel of my clasp it throbbed and vibrated. It was a cord that shook with messages in sea language. I was connected to it. I had tied myself on to the end of it, and now I belonged to the sea. I was cast up on the beach, but the sea could easily pull me back into itself if I just let go, let myself go with the tide. I would float in the wild water, I would be carried close to the sea's heart.

But perhaps it was I who held the cable and did the pulling. Perhaps it was I who would lean back and haul like the fishermen did when they winched up their boats. What had I caught? A sloppy pale blob like a jellyfish, with long tentacles that stung, and an enormous open mouth like a shark's, razor-teeth ready to bite me, to eat me up. As bad as the Alsatian dog who might appear at any moment.

I sat very still in case anything was looking at me. Like in my dream last night. When I watched. It woke me up, and I found I'd wet the bed. It just washed through me, I couldn't stop it, rushing and warm, then I woke up cold and stinking. I was so ashamed I started crying. My mother heard me and came down. She found me some clean pyjamas and changed my sheets and put me back to bed. She promised to stay with me until I went back to sleep again. She said I couldn't sleep in her bed.

It had started to drizzle. There was wet trickling down the back of my neck now as well as in the bottom of my boots. I jumped to my feet and shouted for Jeremy.

At the fish stall at the top of the beach I looked at the lobsters, still alive, waving their claws, and chose cod, because it was well dead. The fisherman wrapped it up for me in a sheet of newspaper, a damp parcel smelling of the sea. I tucked it under my arm and went to collect my bundle of driftwood.

The front door, unlatched, swung open easily, like the door of my parents' room in my dream last night. My father must have walked off his bad temper and come home. I put the fish on the larder shelf, dumped the wood next to the boiler where Jeremy was already settled in his basket, and went to look for my parents in the studio.

They weren't there, though the oil heater was on. My father had been tidying up. He'd washed all his brushes and pots and laid them out neatly on the big shelf under the window. There was still dust everywhere, and paint splashes thick on the lino, and bits of wood, paper and canvas littering the corners. I knew what he meant when he said he liked working in a bit of a mess. It made him feel comfortable.

Now he was teasing my mother about housework. I could hear his voice booming through the sitting-room door. I stood in the doorway and watched them.

My giant father was lying on the sofa in front of the fireplace reading the newspaper. He was so long, lying down, that his feet hung over the end. My mother was scuttling about impatiently emptying ashtrays, throwing dead flowers into the fire, plumping up cushions. Her hair stood up in spikes as though she'd been running her fingers through it. I saw my father eyeing it.

– What's for lunch? he was roaring: I'm starving, woman. Do I have to do everything myself?

He was laughing and now so was she. She shook the crumbs off the hearthrug into the fire. In just the time I'd been standing at the door she'd made the place look welcoming again. She turned towards him and saw me. She advanced on me and picked me up in her strong arms, and I swung, loose and collapsed as a jellyfish, between her hands.

From *During Mother's Absence*, published by Virago.

tHe company of woLves

ANGELA CARTER

One beast and only one howls in the woods by night.

The wolf is carnivore incarnate and he's as cunning as he is ferocious; once he's had a taste of flesh then nothing else will do.

At night, the eyes of wolves shine like candle flames, yellowish, reddish, but that is because the pupils of their eyes fatten on darkness and catch the light from your lantern to flash it back to you – red for danger; if a wolf's eyes reflect only moonlight, then they gleam a cold and unnatural green, a mineral, a piercing colour. If the benighted traveller spies those luminous, terrible sequins stitched suddenly on the black thickets, then he knows he must run, if fear has not struck him stock-still.

But those eyes are all you will be able to glimpse of the forest assassins as they cluster invisibly round your smell of meat as you go through the wood unwisely late. They will be like shadows, they will be like wraiths, grey members of a congregation of nightmare; hark! his long, wavering howl ...an aria of fear made audible.

The wolfsong is the sound of the rending you will suffer, in itself a murdering.

It is winter and cold weather. In this region of mountain and forest, there is now nothing for the wolves to eat. Goats and sheep are locked up in the byre, the deer departed for the remaining pasturage on the southern slopes – wolves grow lean and famished. There is so little flesh on them that you could count the starveling ribs through their pelts, if they gave you time before they pounced. Those slavering jaws; the lolling tongue; the rime of saliva on the grizzled chops – of all the teeming perils of the night and the forest, ghosts, hobgoblins, ogres that grill babies upon gridirons, witches that fatten their captives in cages for cannibal tables, the wolf is worst for he cannot listen to reason.

You are always in danger in the forest, where no people are. Step between the portals of the great pines where the shaggy branches tangle about you, trapping the unwary traveller in nets as if the vegetation itself were in a plot with the wolves who live there, as though the wicked trees go fishing on behalf of their friends – step between the gateposts of the forest with the greatest trepidation and infinite precautions, for if you stray from the path for one instant, the wolves will eat you. They are grey as famine, they are as unkind as plague.

The grave-eyed children of the sparse villages always carry knives with them when they go to tend the little flocks of goats that provide the homesteads with acrid milk and rank, maggoty cheese. Their knives are half as big as they are, the blades are sharpened daily.

But the wolves have ways of arriving at your own hearthside. We try and try but sometimes we cannot keep them out. There is no winter's night the cottager does not fear to see a lean, grey, famished snout questing under the door, and there was a woman once bitten in her own kitchen as she was straining the macaroni.

Fear and flee the wolf; for, worst of all, the wolf may be more than he seems.

There was a hunter once, near here, that trapped a wolf in a pit. This wolf had massacred the sheep and goats; eaten up a mad old man who used to live by himself in a hut halfway up the mountain and sing to Jesus all day; pounced on a girl looking after the sheep, but she made such a commotion that men came with rifles and scared him away and tried to track him to the forest but he was cunning and easily gave them the slip. So this hunter dug a pit and put a duck in it, for bait, all alive-oh; and he covered the pit with straw smeared with wolf dung. Quack, quack! went the duck and a wolf came slinking out of the forest, a big one, a heavy one, he weighed as much as a grown man and the straw gave way beneath him – into the pit he tumbled. The hunter jumped down after him, slit his throat, cut off all his paws for a trophy.

And then no wolf at all lay in front of the hunter but the bloody trunk of a man, headless, footless, dying, dead.

A witch from up the valley once turned an entire wedding party into wolves because the groom had settled on another girl. She used to order them to visit her, at night, from spite, and they would sit and howl around her cottage for her, serenading her with their misery.

Not so very long ago, a young woman in our village married a man who vanished clean away on her wedding night. The bed was made with new sheets and the bride lay down in it; the groom said, he was going out to relieve himself, insisted on it, for the sake of decency, and she drew the coverlet up to her chin and lay there. And she waited and she waited and then she waited again – surely he's been gone a long time? Until she jumps up in bed and shrieks to hear a howling, coming on the wind from the forest.

That long-drawn, wavering howl has, for all its fearful resonance, some inherent sadness in it, as if the beasts would love to be less beastly if only they knew how and never cease to mourn their own condition. There is a vast melancholy in the canticles of the wolves, melancholy infinite as the forest, endless as these long nights of winter and yet that ghastly sadness, that mourning for their own, irremediable appetites, can never move the heart for not one phrase in it hints at the possibility of redemption; grace could not come to the wolf from its own despair, only through some external mediator, so that, sometimes, the beast will look as if he half welcomes the knife that dispatches him.

The young woman's brothers searched the outhouses and the haystacks but never found any remains so the sensible girl dried her eyes and found herself another husband not too shy to piss into a pot who spent the nights indoors. She gave him a pair of bonny babies and all went right as a trivet until, one freezing night, the night of the solstice, the hinge of the year when things do not fit together as well as they should, the longest night, her first good man came home again.

A great thump on the door announced him as she was stirring the soup for the father of her children and she knew him the moment she lifted the latch to him although it was years since she'd worn black for him and now he was in rags and his hair hung down his back and never saw a comb, alive with lice.

'Here I am again, missus,' he said. 'Get me my bowl of cabbage and be quick about it.'

Then her second husband came in with wood for the fire and when the first one saw she'd slept with another man and, worse, clapped his red eyes on her little children who'd crept into the kitchen to see what all the din was about, he shouted: 'I wish I were a wolf again, to teach this whore a lesson!' So a wolf he instantly became and tore off the eldest boy's left foot before he was chopped by the hatchet they used for chopping logs. But when the wolf lay bleeding and gasping its last, the pelt peeled off again and he was just as he had been, years ago, when he ran away from his marriage bed, so that she wept and her second husband beat her.

They say there's an ointment the Devil gives you that turns you into a wolf the minute you rub it on. Or, that he was born feet first and had a wolf for his father and his torso is a man's but his legs and genitals are a wolf's. And he has a wolf's heart.

Seven years is a werewolf's natural span but if you burn his human clothes you condemn him to wolfishness for the rest of his life, so old wives hereabouts think it some protection to throw a hat or an apron at the werewolf, as if clothes made the man. Yet by the eyes, those phosphorescent eyes, you know him in all his shapes; the eyes alone unchanged by metamorphosis.

Before he can become a wolf, the lycanthrope strips stark naked. If you spy a naked man among the pines, you must run as if the Devil were after you.

It is midwinter and the robin, the friend of man, sits on the handle of the gardener's spade and sings. It is the worst time in all the year for wolves but this strong-minded child insists she will go off through the wood. She is quite sure the wild beasts cannot harm her although, well-warned, she lays a carving knife in the basket her mother has packed with cheeses. There is a bottle of harsh liquor distilled from brambles; a batch of flat oatcakes baked on the heathstone; a pot or two of jam. The girl will take these delicious gifts to a reclusive grandmother so old the burden of her years is crushing her to death. Granny lives two hours' trudge through the winter woods; the child wraps herself up in her thick shawl, draws it over her head. She steps into her stout wooden shoes; she is dressed and ready and it is Christmas Eve. The malign door of the solstice still swings upon its hinges but she has been too much loved ever to feel scared.

Children do not stay young for long in this savage country. There are no toys for them to play with so they work hard and grow wise but this one, so pretty and the youngest of her family, a little late-comer, had been indulged by her mother and the grandmother who'd knitted her the red shawl that, today, has the ominous if brilliant look of blood on snow. Her breasts have just begun to swell; her hair is like lint, so fair it hardly makes a shadow on her pale forehead; her cheeks are an emblematic scarlet and white and she just started her woman's bleeding, the clock inside her that will strike, henceforward, once a month.

She stands and moves within the visible pentacle of her own

virginity. She is an unbroken egg; she is a sealed vessel; she has inside her a magic space the entrance to which is shut tight with a plug of membrane; she is a closed system; she does not know how to shiver. She has her knife and she is afraid of nothing.

Her father might forbid her, if he were home, but he is away in the forest, gathering wood, and her mother cannot deny her.

The forest closed upon her like a pair of jaws.

There is always something to look at in the forest, even in the middle of winter – the huddled mounds of birds, succumbed to the lethargy of the season, heaped on the creaking boughs and too forlorn to sing; the bright frills of the winter fungi on the blotched trunks of the trees; the cuneiform slots of rabbits and deer, the herringbone tracks of the birds, a hare as lean as a rasher of bacon streaking across the path where the thin sunlight dapples the russet brakes of last year's bracken.

When she heard the freezing howl of a distant wolf, her practised hand sprang to the handle of her knife, but she saw no sign of a wolf at all, nor of a naked man, neither, but then she heard a clattering among the brushwood and there sprang on to the path a fully clothed one, a very handsome young one, in the green coat and wideawake hat of a hunter, laden with carcasses of game birds. She had her hand on her knife at the first rustle of twigs but he laughed with a flash of white teeth when he saw her and made her a comic yet flattering little bow; she'd never seen such a fine fellow before, not among the rustic clowns of her native village. So on they went, through the thickening light of the afternoon.

Soon they were laughing and joking like old friends. When he offered to carry her basket, she gave it to him although her knife was in it because he told her his rifle would protect them. As the day darkened, it began to snow again; she felt the first flakes settle on her eyelashes but now there was only half a mile to go and there would be a fire, and hot tea, and a welcome, a warm one surely, for the dashing huntsman as well as for herself.

This young man had a remarkable object in his pocket. It was a compass. She looked at the little round glassface in the palm of his hand and watched the wavering needle with a vague wonder. He assured her this compass had taken him safely through the wood on his hunting trip because the needle always told him with perfect accuracy where the north was. She did not believe it; she knew she should never leave the path on the way through the wood or else she would be lost instantly. He laughed at her again; gleaming trails of spittle clung to his teeth. He said, if he plunged off the path into the forest that surrounded them, he would guarantee to arrive at her grandmother's house a good quarter of an hour before she did, plotting his way through the undergrowth with his compass, while she trudged the long way, along the winding path.

I don't believe you. Besides, aren't you afraid of the wolves?

He only tapped the gleaming butt of his rifle and grinned.

Is it a bet? he asked her. Shall we make a game of it? What will you give me if I get to your grandmother's house before you?

What would you like? she asked disingenuously.

A kiss.

Commonplaces of a rustic seduction; she lowered her eyes and blushed.

He went through the undergrowth and took her basket with him but she forgot to be afraid of the beasts, although now the moon was rising, for she wanted to dawdle on her way to make sure the handsome gentleman would win his wager.

Grandmother's house stood by itself a little way out of the village. The freshly falling snow blew in eddies about the kitchen garden and the young man stepped delicately up the snowy path to the door as if he were reluctant to get his feet wet, swinging his bundle of game and the girl's basket and humming a little tune to himself.

There is a faint trace of blood on his chin; he has been snacking on his catch.

He rapped upon the panels with his knuckles.

Aged and frail, granny is three-quarters succumbed to the mortality the ache in her bones promises her and almost ready to give in entirely. A boy came out from the village to build up her hearth for the night an hour ago and the kitchen crackles with busy firelight. She has her Bible for company, she is a pious old woman. She is propped up on several pillows in the bed set into the wall peasant-fashion, wrapped up in the patchwork quilt she made before she was married, more years ago than she cares to remember. Two china spaniels with liver-coloured blotches on their coats and black noses sit on either side of the fireplace. There is a bright rug of woven rags on the pantiles. The grandfather clock ticks away her eroding time.

We keep the wolves outside by living well.

He rapped upon the panels with his hairy knuckles.

It is your granddaughter, he mimicked in a high soprano.

Lift up the latch and walk in, my darling.

You can tell them by their eyes, eyes of a beast of prey, nocturnal, devastating eyes as red as a wound; you can hurl your Bible at him and your apron after, granny, you thought that was a sure prophylactic against these infernal vermin . . . now call on Christ and his mother and all the angels in heaven to protect you but it won't do you any good.

His feral muzzle is sharp as a knife; he drops his golden burden of gnawed pheasant on the table and puts down her dear girl's basket, too. Oh, my God, what have you done with her?

Off with his disguise, that coat of forest-coloured cloth, the hat with the feather tucked into the ribbon; his matted hair streams down his white shirt and she can see the lice moving in it. The sticks in the hearth shift and hiss; night and the forest has come into the kitchen with darkness tangled in its hair.

He strips off his shirt. His skin is the colour and texture of vellum. A crisp stripe of hair runs down his belly. his nipples are ripe and dark as poison fruit but he's so thin you could count the ribs under his skin if only he gave you the time. He strips off his trousers and she can see how hairy his legs are. His genitals, huge. Ah! huge.

The last thing the old lady saw in all this world was a young man, eyes like cinders, naked as a stone, approaching her bed.

The wolf is carnivore incarnate.

When he had finished with her, he licked his chops and quickly dressed himself again, until he was just as he had been when he came through her door. He burned the inedible hair in the fireplace and wrapped the bones up in a napkin that he hid away under the bed in the wooden chest in which he found a clean pair of sheets. These he carefully put on the bed instead of the tell-tale stained ones he stowed away in the laundry basket. He plumped up the pillows and shook out the patchwork quilt, he picked up the Bible from the floor, closed it and laid it on the table. All was as it had been before except that grandmother was gone. The sticks twitched in the grate, the clock ticked and the young man sat patiently, deceitfully beside the bed in granny's nightcap.

Rat-a-tap-tap.

Who's there, he quavers in granny's antique falsetto.

Only your granddaughter.

So she came in, bringing with her a flurry of snow that melted in tears on the tiles, and perhaps she was a little disappointed to see only her grandmother sitting beside the fire. But then he flung off the blanket and sprang to the door, pressing his back against it so that she could not get out again.

The girl looked round the room and saw there was not even the indentation of a head on the smooth cheek of the pillow and how, for the first time she'd seen it so, the Bible lay closed on the table. The tick of the clock cracked like a whip. She wanted her knife from her basket but she did not dare to reach for it because his eyes were fixed upon her – huge eyes that now seemed to shine with a unique, interior light, eyes the size of saucers, saucers full of Greek fire, diabolic phosphorescence.

What big eyes you have.

All the better to see you with.

No trace at all of the old woman except for a turf of white hair that had caught in the bark of an unburned log. When the girl saw that, she knew she was in danger of death.

Where is my grandmother?

There's nobody here but we two, my darling.

Now a great howling rose up all around them, near, very near, as close as the kitchen garden, the howling of a multitude of wolves; she knew the worst wolves are hairy on the inside and she shivered, in spite of the scarlet shawl she pulled more closely round herself as if it could protect her although it was as red as the blood she must spill.

Who has come to sing us carols, she said.

Those are the voices of my brothers, darling; I love the company of wolves. Look out of the window and you'll see them.

Snow half-caked the lattice and she opened it to look into the garden. It was a white night of moon and snow; the blizzard whirled round the gaunt, grey beasts who squatted on their haunches among the rows of winter cabbage, pointing their sharp snouts to the moon and howling as if their hearts would break. Ten wolves; twenty wolves – so many wolves she could not count them, howling in concert as if demented or deranged. Their eyes reflected the light from the kitchen and shone like a hundred candles.

It is very cold, poor things, she said; no wonder they howl so.

She closed the window on the wolves' threnody and took off her scarlet shawl, the colour of poppies, the colour of sacrifices, the colour of her menses, and, since her fear did her no good, she ceased to be afraid.

What shall I do with my shawl?

Throw it on the fire, dear one. You won't need it again.

She bundled up her shawl and threw it on the blaze, which instantly consumed it. Then she drew her blouse over her head; her small breasts gleamed as if the snow had invaded the room.

What shall I do with my blouse?

Into the fire with it too, my pet.

The thin muslin went flaring up the chimney like a magic bird and now off came her skirt, her woollen stockings, her shoes, and on to the fire they went, too, and were gone for good. The firelight shone through the edges of her skin; now she was clothed only in her untouched integument of flesh. This dazzling, naked she combed out her hair with her fingers; her hair looked white as the snow outside. Then went directly to the man with red eyes in whose unkempt mane the lice moved; she stood up on tiptoe and unbuttoned the collar of his shirt.

What big arms you have.

All the better to hug you with.

Every wolf in the world now howled a prothalamion outside the window as she freely gave him the kiss she owed him.

What big teeth you have!

She saw how his jaw began to slaver and the room was full of the clamour of the forest's *Liebestod* but the wise child never flinched, even as he answered: All the better to eat you with.

The girl burst out laughing; she knew she was nobody's meat. She laughed at him full in the face, she ripped off his shirt for him and flung it into the fire, in the fiery wake of her own discarded clothing. The flames danced like dead souls on Walpursignacht and the old bones under the bed set up a terrible clattering but she did not pay them any heed.

Carnivore incarnate, only immaculate flesh appeases him.

She will lay his fearful head on her lap and she will pick out the lice from his pelt and perhaps she will put the lice into her mouth and eat them, as he will bid her, as she would do in a savage marriage ceremony.

The blizzard will die down.

The blizzard died down, leaving the mountains as randomly covered with snow as if a blind woman had thrown a sheet over them, the upper branches of the forest pines limed, creaking, swollen with the fall.

Snowlight, moonlight, a confusion of paw-prints.

All silent, all silent.

Midnight; the clock strikes. It is Christmas day, the werewolves' birthday, the door of the solstice stands wide open; let them all sink through.

See! sweet and sound she sleeps in granny's bed, between the paws of the tender wolf.

From *The Bloody Chamber*, published by Penguin.

cap o'rushes

A.L. KENNEDY

It was Christmas and they all had flu. Her husband, her children, herself; they all had flu. It first affected their heads and then it gripped across their chests and, finally, it settled on their stomachs. It made them sick.

She rolled from her side to her back and out of the shape of warmth her lying had left. The new stretch of sheet was just cool enough to be nice.

She thought.

Why had they done it this year? Why had they bothered?

For the children.

But the boys had known what their presents would be in November. There was no surprise. They didn't even like Christmas things: not turkey, or stuffing, or sprouts. No one had felt like eating in any case. The television was awful, they'd seen all the films before on video and they missed their friends from school as soon as the holiday came. Too sick to get away from each other and too well not to care, they sniped and yapped across their room, spilled Ribena in their beds and coughed until they gagged and threw up.

'He was eating my hair gel.'
  'No I was not. You'd have to be stupid to eat hair gel.'
  'So you are stupid.'
  'Not as stupid as you are for wearing it. Poof.'
  'Bastard.'
  'Fanny.'
  'Poof yourself.'

When she was young, her mother read her stories and she'd liked them. Not because she was a little girl, but because she was a little human being. Then she'd read the stories to herself and that was even better. One Sunday morning, she'd woken up, before the birds or the sun, and run to stand and yell in her parents' bedroom.
  'I can read! I can read!'
  She hadn't realised before.
  But now there were centuries and libraries and whole generations of books that belonged to her. Because she could read. She knew their secrets. No one had been as pleased as she was on that Sunday: her mother and father had known she could read for months and had looked at her very strangely, once they were fully awake. Her mother had shouted, but inside, she had probably been pleased. About the reading.
  Neither of the boys liked books. They preferred Graphic Novels with pretentious subtexts and violence and sex. She often asked them why they only read comics. When she said this, they would smirk and roll their eyes.
  Occasionally, thinking of the books she'd read when she was a little girl, she would look at her sons and see how alien they were. Little boys, little human beings, they liked books. But she had two little changelings. Two little goblin sons.
  Then again, she'd married a goblin, so what else could she expect?
  In the privacy of her head, her family were The Goblins.

That was their name. She couldn't remember deciding, but there it was. No other name could suit them so well. And, because of the terrible flu, the Goblin King and his Goblin Children had gone to their Goblin Grandmother in the West. Such nasty flu. They wouldn't be back for five whole days. Five was her lucky number.

It was fully half past ten before she got up. She had a bath. From the warm of the sheets, to the hot of the bath, to the shiveriness of the underwear and blouse. Having added a skirt and sweater, she made brunch. She felt hungry and better, relaxed.

While she washed up – which somehow she didn't mind doing, just for herself – she ran over her Goblin Lore. She thought of The Signs.

HOW TO TELL YOUR HUSBAND IS A GOBLIN.

She smiled. Colin was a goblin because it was obvious he was a goblin and once you knew he was a goblin, you couldn't think otherwise. There weren't really signs. Nothing infallible. She could have asked her mother what she thought but the answer to the question, 'Is Colin the famous Goblin King of myth and legend?' would have been the same as the answer to 'Will he turn out to be a pervert once I've married him?' or 'Will I regret this decision for the rest of my life?' or 'Is this man an ex-Nazi war criminal, clinging to a double existence as an axe murderer and merchant of child pornography?'

'Yes.'

'Yes.'

'Yes.'

'Yes. Isn't it obvious?'

Mothers never liked their prospective sons-in-law. Not true. Her mother never liked Colin. That was true.

If there was anything which had convinced her that Colin was the Goblin King, then it was probably his shirts. She might as well settle for that.

His shirts, even very new shirts, not yet washed, would

change when he put them on. The layers that made up his collars would bubble and peel away from each other, like paint on an old door. His cuffs would ravel and fray while the cloth beneath his armpits yellowed permanently. Clothing seemed to decompose around him and within hours it would seem he had brought it from his grave.

There was something about him rotten. Rotting.

She could imagine his mother receiving him each night from school: scolding and mending and scrubbing away, fighting to send him out in the morning looking as though he was cared for. Had she ever considered there might be something wrong? With him, instead of her? Or had she been a goblin, too.

You couldn't tell now, because she was dead.

She noticed, with the house only free of goblins for one night, it already smelled entirely different. It wasn't that you noticed much while they were there, but there was definitely something missing, now they were gone. There was something they had taken away. In the corners of the rooms, she could still disturb it, as she gathered in their dust: the smell of earth and gravel, damp places and decay. As soon as Colin left, she'd changed their bed and when she woke this morning, she could breathe easily and she felt clean. She usually had a thick head in the mornings.

Her five days passed more slowly than she'd thought. There was time for personal shopping with a lunch in town and she went to the pictures twice; looking at the mothers and fathers with their human, little daughters and sons. She bought books – a great many – more than she'd bought in years and she started to read them carefully, rolling the words round her head to see how they tasted. Night and morning she had a bath, used talcum and perfume, and every day the house grew cleaner and more fragrant along with her. She planted new window boxes and wished it was Spring outside.

The sun set on the fifth day and the rain misted down and she found herself listening for cars in the street below. Almost without thinking, she hid her books away and set four dishes warming, ready for the stew. The goblins were always hungry and always arrived when a meal was on the way. They had very good noses for soups and gravies, in the same way that sharks were sensitive to blood.

The goblin feet stumped on the stair, two pairs of light stumps and one pair that were heavy, and the door was opened with the Goblin King's key. She felt her stomach tighten and knew that if she wasn't careful, her hands would shake.

Years ago, when she had first met Colin, the symptoms had been the same. Waiting in cafés, or on corners, watching for his head to waver above the crowd, she had been equally tense. She had never been sure, when he took her hand, if she smiled because she loved him, or because she knew he wouldn't see her tremble, now that he had her gripped. She didn't know why she was nervous now, except that it was something he shouldn't find out.

It wasn't unusual that she picked at her food. Visitors who saw the goblins eating often had no appetite at all. Colin's jaws would slap together and suck apart, answered by miniature slaps and sucks from his sons. They didn't eat; they consumed. Forks, hands, spoons, were filled, scraps pursued, juices sopped. The mouths were always open, anxious, grim.

She thought she remembered mentioning this to Colin. She thought she remembered him laughing. She thought she remembered him talking about the manly approach to food. This was how men ate. He was bringing his sons up to eat like men. She didn't want them to enjoy their food?

How could she stop them enjoying their food? Goblins always did.

After dinner, the goblins grew drowsy. The blood rushed to their stomachs from their brains and they liked to sprawl in the sitting room for television and sleep. Colin would stay quite quiet until bedtime, but his sons would normally settle for an hour or so and then begin to fret and squirm. Tonight the journey had tired them and they were peaceful.

She washed up and came through to join them, noticing,

when she opened the door, that the room now smelt like a cave as she walked in. A cave where someone had recently spilt gravy.

The curtains were tight drawn and only the dead blue glow from the television lit the room. She sat in the armchair facing Colin, watching him. He looked heavy. Stony, in fact. Composed of stones. The hands were broad, flattened by their weight across his knees. They were asleep. His head was only dozing yet, set deep between his shoulders, keeping steady for his eyes and letting them flicker about, or stare, or close.

His eyes were almost closed now, so she could examine him safely. She wondered how he might look on television. How would they present him? Sitting amongst rocks, or feeding, scooping water from a stream? Perhaps mating: they always showed you that. Would other people see him and find him likeable, or would they be aware of that certain strangeness? She thought they would notice the strangeness. Goblins looked very like people, but somehow that made their differences all the more clear. They were disturbing.

Because five was her lucky number she stayed with the goblins another five weeks.

Then on a Sunday evening, driving, driving through the last of the countryside before the city's light turned into streets, Colin inclined his head a little and asked,

'Well now boys, let's see. How much do you love me today, then, eh? How much? James first.'

'Aw, but Jimmy's always first.'

'That's right. How much do you love me, Jimmy? How much do you love your rotten old dad?'

'Loads. Loads and loads. Honest. I love you more than he does.'

'No you don't.'

'So how much do you love me, William?'

'I love you mountains full. I love you more than anyone else in the whole world.'

'More than anyone at all?'

'Yeah. You're brilliant, Dad. Totally brilliant.'

'Thank you, William.'

'I think you're brilliant, too.'

'I thought he was brilliant.'

'So did I, I just didn't say it.'

'Liar.'

'Fanny.'

'Prick.'

'Boys, boys.'

'He is so a prick.'

'Yes, but you mustn't call him that in front of ladies, William. And your mother is a lady.'

'William got it wrong again.'

'Aye, but at least I'm no a prick.'

She thought that would be the end of it. Usually the end to most of their family discussions was like this. But Colin made the boys be quiet again.

'Boys, be quiet again. As there is a lady present, we should ask her the question, too. What do you think?'

'Aye, go on, Dad.'

'Aye, go on.'

'Hmm? So what do you say, wee wifie, how much do you love your old man? How much?'

'Say mountains, mum.'

'Say he's brilliant.'

'Brilliant was my word. Prick.'

She paused to look out of the window. The city was almost upon them now, it wouldn't be long. She saw her face, flat over fields; a string of bungalows; a bridge. She let Colin realise that he was waiting, that she had made him wait, and then she watched her face smile as she told him.

'As much as I can. I love you as much as I can.'

There was no other choice but to go, once that had happened. The Goblin King agreed with her on that.

*

36

The office was very nice. When she went there for the interview, she'd liked it. There were posters and lists in marker pen all around the walls and drawings from somebody's child behind one of the desks. On the window ledge there were geraniums: yellow and very leggy, but geraniums all the same.

They'd known that her typing was rusty. She also told them that she'd been married and hadn't worked for several years. The woman asking her questions had looked very serious at that. Then she had explained that all the other applicants for the job had been decidedly inexperienced and that the office was in need of someone a little more dependable.

'You mean older.'

'No. Dependable. But I won't say your age wouldn't be an advantage. People tend not to trust this kind of organisation – if the first person they meet is a twenty-year-old in tie-dyed pyjamas who can't remember where the diary went...'

'I think I know what you mean.'

'She means you'll be our front man. So all of the tie-dyed pyjamas brigade can run amok to themselves in peace.'

The voice came from a man in jeans and a sweatshirt, perched on the corner of a desk beside the window. He held his hand across the mouthpiece of the telephone and smiled, nodding to whatever he was hearing from along the line.

He didn't look like a goblin, but you can never tell.

Colin hadn't known she had a job waiting when she went. He probably hadn't thought it was possible. But it had been. And she had rented a place near the river: two rooms, a kitchen and a bathroom, sectioned out of a large, sandstone house. The newer, thinner walls sounded hollow and frail and the furniture the landlord provided was very tired, but it was fine for now. It smelt of human beings.

When it was finally the last time she would see it, leaving the Goblin's house had been hard. It had been her house, too. And it was warm and comfortable, with nice carpets and ornaments; bits and pieces she had chosen and liked. She arrived in the new place and sat on the rusty sofa, her bags still by the door. She cried a little. Then she unpacked what familiar scents and colours she'd brought with her. She put a sweater to her face, breathing it in, and cried again. But the rooms did change. While she was out at work, something seemed to spread from her books and pictures and, after a month or so, she could come home and not feel a chill of strangeness. Just make a cup of coffee and rest her back.

It was the typing that stiffened her back. She wasn't used to it at all and by lunch time on a busy day, her neck and shoulders would feel almost bruised.

'Just because you're the new girl, you don't have to work too hard. Relax. It's the only way you'll survive in here.'

This time the man was in his shirtsleeves. Still jeans. His smile hadn't changed.

He was far too young, though. Indecently young.

'Don't worry, Ben, I'm alright.'

'Not as green as you're cabbage looking, eh?'

'Something like that.'

'Well, I'll leave you to get on with it.'

'Hmmm.'

She absorbed herself in the pattern of words on her paper until she could feel him drift away.

He was right, of course, she did know what she was doing. She was making herself indispensable. Not that it was very hard. Everyone at the office needed her to be that way.

'Oh, you saved my life. I couldn't think where I'd left it. Thanks again.'

'Could you speak to him. Explain that dancers can't dance on a concrete floor. Their legs break. He'll listen to you.'

'And this is our wonderful secretary. She tells us all where we should be and who we should be with and what we should be doing. Everything. Really. The place couldn't run without her now.'

*

She smiled when they said these things. She knew they believed they were lying, flattering, but really what they were saying was true. They weren't efficient, so she was. Not too much to be threatening and always very patient, but efficient, too. They wanted to be mothered and organised and to tell their problems to someone they didn't have to know.

They didn't know her. She made sure of that. It was a strength.

In return for their very generous and frequent compliments, she allowed herself to be mystified by their work. She would look at the pots and pictures in their little gallery space, the peculiarly jumbled black and white photographs and she would say nothing. Not even a word. Perhaps she would shake her head, gently, before she went back to her files, but that would be all.

Some of the things were actually very nice, but it wouldn't do to tell the artists that. She had to keep them guessing, because that was a strength.

The year is still young
when you are here my one love
green will always show

It was the second poem she'd found on her desk. The first hadn't been very good. This was alright, but not amazing.

She knew who it was from. The young one in the jeans. She wanted to go over and tell him. The year is still young because it's April, it has nothing to do with me. She wanted to thank him for putting his verses in envelopes so that no one else knew they were there and to ask if perhaps from now on he could just leave the envelopes and dispense with the poetry. Envelopes were useful, after all.

He circled towards her desk and she typed.

He sat and wheeled himself towards her in an office chair and she typed.

'Could I just interrupt a minute?'

She glanced up and checked the collar of his shirt. It wasn't new, but it was clean and perfectly smooth. Not a goblin.

'Of course you can. What is it?'

'I wondered what you thought of the poems. I know you read poetry, I've seen you do it. I mean, I like the photography and it just about earns me a living, but I want to write. It's difficult finding someone you can show things to.'

'Embarrassing.'

'I thought you'd understand.'

'Well, we should talk about it sometime. Come round and have tea. Would that be nice?'

Tea was nice and motherly, it wouldn't scare him. Apparently, he needed not to be scared. 'I wondered what you thought of the poems.' Was that serious? What should she tell him? You may not be a goblin, but your poetry is dreadful and your chat-up lines are worse?

Besides which, who would send you anonymous poems on love and then explain they were only literature? He didn't seem to notice that was insulting.

She continued with her typing. When she was into the flow of it, the words lined across the paper, as if she was rubbing the whiteness away; not putting a blackness on. She was squeezing the words out from where they were already hiding. That was a comfortable idea. It had nothing to do with the sense of what she wrote, nothing to do with reality at all and it meant that she couldn't be wrong, because she was only finding something, not inventing it. She didn't know if she wanted the feeling this gave her, but it stopped her from making spelling mistakes.

The tea was planned for Sunday, which made it Sunday Tea. She bought an oily cherry cake and a tea pot. She hadn't bothered with a pot, just for herself.

The flat the young man arrived at was still quite new to her. In a red sandstone tenement, with solid walls, it had suited her before she moved in and now it suited her more. The rent was high, but she was managing. When he stepped into the hall, across one of her new rugs, he was obviously impressed. Surprised.

'You do read a lot, don't you?'

The hall was lined with cheap bookshelves, all filled. She was proud of them all.

'I might just like the way they fill the space. I might not have read even one.' She smiled and led him into the living room, made him sit down.

She had already decided how the afternoon would go. It wouldn't.

Sending her poems like that. He annoyed her in the same way the office annoyed her. Both of them imagined they were outside reality. She always enjoyed her stories and fairy tales, but she didn't want them all the time. It felt like living with the Goblins – it stifled her breath.

'So, about your poems, Ben. If I can call you Ben.'

'Sure, sure. I'm sorry, nobody seems to call you by your name. I don't know it.'

'Nobody knows it. It's a private thing.'

'Oh.'

'You must have read the old stories. If you give someone your name, you're giving them power over you. It's funny how few people notice.'

'Yes.'

'Who are you writing to? In the poems. Who are they to?'

'No one. No one in particular. I thought that would be better. Whoever read them could think it was someone they knew. Anyone. A woman. A man.'

'A parrot.'

'What?'

'I mean, they feel anonymous. They're very warm, but they're very anonymous.'

'I see.'

'They'll probably do very well.'

'I'm sorry?'

'Look over there, in the corner. You gave me the idea. For want of a better description, they're tie-dyed pyjamas and little hats.'

'Whose are they?'

'I don't know yet. I make them and sell them. I do quite well. The first ones, I gave to the students who stayed in my old place. I vary the design and the cloth is always different. Sometimes I prepare it, sometimes art students. To be accurate, it's printing, not tie-dye.'

'Wonderful. I never knew.'

'It's not wonderful. It's rubbish. They sell for four or five times what they cost to make; they fit no one; they're garish and poorly sewn. We live in a cold, wet city and these are as thin as handkerchiefs and just about as warm; they're criminal. But I can sell them and I can make money. They're anonymous, too, so they sell.

'I ran away from my husband and now I make clothes by a river. I even put a little label inside them: "Cap O'Rushes", do you see? Like the woman in the story.'

'Yes, I remember it.'

'I thought you would. Ask anyone in that office and probably they would – it would be their style. Ask them what was in the paper yesterday and they wouldn't have a clue. Beggars and wizards and wise old men: we have beggars now, do they know that?'

'Of course, you can't avoid them.'

'Yes, you can. If you couldn't avoid them, they wouldn't still be there.'

'Cap O'Rushes went back to her husband – will you do that?'

'What do you think?'

'I don't think you'll stick to the plot.'

'Well no, neither do I.'

'But I should stick to photographs, right?'

'It isn't up to me. You should maybe write stories, or plays, or maybe your poems are terrific and I wasn't the right person to ask.'

'I thought you didn't like stories.'

'I do like stories. But they're only by dead people – you couldn't compete.'

For the rest of the afternoon, they talked like human beings.

42

She refreshed the tea pot and told him her name. Being careful was one thing, but sometimes, she could border on the eccentric. She was sad when he had to go, but a little relieved, so he must have left at about the right time.

When the evening began to darken, she drew the curtains and sat back in the corner of the sofa, her shoes off and her feet curled underneath her. She was so relaxed. She had been all day. If she had a good, female friend she could have told her how relaxing it was for an apparently single woman to finally know that she didn't have to care. They would have laughed and then been serious about that. There was no need to lean on an absent boyfriend, or a husband. People could think she was gay, or frigid, or mad, or whatever they wanted, it didn't matter. She was enough in herself, which made her confident, which made her enough in herself. That was very good. A real strength.

She wished it hadn't taken her so many years to be strong.

It was odd that Ben had asked her if she would go back to Colin and the boys. In the story, she should have waited, for example, five years, because that was her lucky number and she would have gone back in disguise.

Fuck that.

If she did ever run into Colin, she would tell him that she did still love him as much as she could. And now she knew how much she could. She had stretched and grown into work and business, happiness and her own home. She knew who she was and that she was capable of as much as she wanted to be. That was very nice.

The thing about Colin was that she still only loved him as much as she could. And that still wasn't very much at all.

It wasn't her fault. No one can ever do more than what they can. It wasn't because he was a goblin, either; she wouldn't need to tell him stories about that. She simply couldn't find him lovable. That was the truth and that was all.

She felt, now, she was finished with all that.

From *Night Geometry and the Garscadden Trains*, published by Polygon.

HACK WEDNESDAY

MARGARET ATWOOD

Marcia has been dreaming about babies. She dreams there is a new one, hers, milky-smelling and sweet-faced and shining with light, lying in her arms, bundled in a green knitted blanket. It even has a name, something strange that she doesn't catch. She is suffused with love, and with longing for it, but then she thinks, Now I will have to take care of it. This wakes her up with a jolt.

Downstairs the news is on. Something extra has happened, she can tell by the announcer's tone of voice, by the heightened energy. A disaster of some kind; that always peps them up. She isn't sure she's ready for it, at least not so early. Not before coffee. She considers the window: a whitish light is coming through it; maybe it's snowing. In any case, it's time to get up again.

Time is going faster and faster; the days of the week whisk by like panties. The panties she's thinking about are the kind she had when she was a little girl, in pastels, with 'Monday', 'Tuesday', 'Wednesday' embroidered on them. Ever since then the days of the week have had colours for her: Monday is blue,

Tuesday is cream, Wednesday is lilac. You counted your way through each week by panty, fresh on each day, then dirtied and thrown into the bin. Marcia's mother used to tell her that she should always wear clean panties in case a bus ran over her, because other people might see them as her corpse was being toted to the morgue. It wasn't Marcia's potential death that loomed uppermost in her mind, it was the state of her panties.

Marcia's mother never actually said this. But it was the kind of thing she ought to have said, because the other mothers really did say it, and it has been a useful story for Marcia. It embodies the supposed Anglo-Canadian prudery, inhibition, and obsession with public opinion, and as such has mythic force. She uses it on foreigners, or on those lately arrived.

Marcia eases herself out of bed and finds the slippers, made from dyed-pink sheepskin, which were given to her last Christmas by her twenty-year-old daughter, out of concern for her aging feet. (Her son, at a loss as usual, gave her chocolates.) She struggles into her dressing gown, which has surely become smaller than it used to be, then gropes through the panty drawer. No embroidery in here, no old-fashioned nylon, even. Romance has given way to comfort, as in much else. She is thankful to God she doesn't live in the age of corsets.

Fully dressed except for the bright pink sheepskin slippers, which she keeps on because of the coldness of the kitchen floor, Marcia makes her way down the stairs and along the hallway. Walking in the slippers, which are slightly too big and flop around, she waddles slightly. Once she was light on her feet, a waif. Now she casts a shadow.

Eric is sitting at the kitchen table having his morning rage. His once red hair, now the colour of bleached-out sand, is standing straight up on his head like a bird's crest, and he's run his hands through it in exasperation. There's marmalade in it again, off his toast.

'Ass-licking suck,' he says. Marcia knows that this is not directed at her: the morning paper is spread all over the table. They cancelled – Eric cancelled – their subscription to this paper five months ago, in a fit of fury over its editorial policies and its failure to use recycled newsprint, although it's the paper Marcia writes her column for. But he can't resist the temptation: every so often he ducks out before Marcia is up and buys one from the corner box. The adrenalin gets him going, now that he's no longer allowed coffee.

Marcia turns down the radio, then kisses the bristly back of his neck. 'What is it today?' she says. 'The benefits of Free Trade?'

There's a tearing sound, like fingernails on a blackboard. Outside the glass kitchen-door, the cat has dug its claws into the screen and is sliding slowly down it. This its demand to be let in. It has never bothered to learn meowing.

'One of these days I'm going to kill that beast,' says Eric. It's Marcia's belief that Eric would never do such a thing, because he is tender-hearted to a fault. Eric's view of himself is more savage.

'You poor baby!' says Marcia, scooping up the cat, which is overweight. It's on a diet, but mooches in secret from the neighbours. Marcia sympathizes.

'I just let the damn thing out. In, out, in out. It can't make up its mind,' says Eric.

'It's confused,' says Marcia. The cat has wriggled free of her. She measures coffee into the little espresso machine. If she were truly loyal to Eric she would give up coffee, too, to spare him the torture of watching her drink it. But then she would be asleep all the time.

'It's picking up on the national mood,' says Eric. 'Yesterday it shat in the bathtub.'

'At least it didn't use the rug,' says Marcia. She peels an envelope of moist cat kibble. The cat rubs up against her legs.

'It would have if it had thought about it,' says Eric. 'Some grovelling hymn to George Bush.' He's back on the editorial page.

'What's he done now?' says Marcia, helping herself to Cheerios. Eric won't eat them because they're American. Ever since the Free Trade deal with the States went through he has refused to purchase anything from south of the border. They've been having a lot of root vegetables this winter: carrots, potatoes, beets. Eric says the pioneers did it, and, anyway, frozen orange juice is overrated. At lunches out, Marcia furtively eats avocados and hopes Eric won't smell them on her breath.

'This is the Panama invasion,' says Eric, distinguishing it from a multitude of other invasions. 'You know how many they're up to this century? Down there? Forty-two.'

'That's a lot,' says Marcia, in her mollifying voice.

'They don't think of it as invading,' says Eric. 'They think of it as agriculture. Sort of like spraying for bugs.'

'Were you cold out there? Did you freeze your paws?' says Marcia, picking up the cat again, which has turned up its nose at the kibble. It gives a pig-like grunt. She's missing the children. Tomorrow they will be home for the holidays, they and their laundry. The children are hers, not hers and Eric's, though even they don't seem to notice this any more. Their real father has become a figment, somewhere in Florida. For Christmas he sends them oranges, which is about all Marcia ever hears of him.

'It's a drug thing,' says Eric. 'They're going to arrest Noriega, and presto, ten thousand poverty-stricken junkies will be cured.'

'He hasn't behaved well,' says Marcia.

'That's not the point,' says Eric.

Marcia sighs. 'I suppose this means you'll be picketing the American Consulate again,' she says.

'Me and a few assorted loonies, and five superannuated Trots,' says Eric. 'Same old bunch.'

'Dress up warm,' says Marcia. 'There's a wind-chill factor.'

'I'll wear my earmuffs,' says Eric: this is his one concession to subzero weather. 'Trots are a nuisance.'

'The Mounties think that *you're* one,' says Marcia.

'Oh, yeah, I forgot – the two Mounties disguised as bag ladies. Or else those jerks from Ca-Sissies. They might as well wear clown suits, they're so obvious.'

Ca-Sissies is Eric's name for CSIS, which really means Canadian Security Intelligence Service. Ca-Sissies taps his phone, or so Eric believes. He teases them: he'll phone up one of his pals and say words like 'sabotage' and 'bomb,' just to activate the tapes. Eric says he's doing Ca-Sissies a favour: he's making them feel important. Marcia says it would interfere with her ever having an affair, because they might listen in and then blackmail her.

Eric is not worried. 'You have good taste,' he says. 'There's no one in this city worth having an affair with.'

Marcia knows that lack of worth has never stopped anyone in this regard. The reason she doesn't have affairs, or hasn't had any lately, is simple laziness. Too much energy is required; also, she no longer has the body for it, for the initial revelations and displays. She would not have an affair without doing something about her thighs, and buying appropriate underwear. In addition, she would not risk losing Eric. Eric can still surprise her, in many ways. She knows the general format of the schemes he's likely to come up with, but not the details. Surprise is worth a lot.

'Love is blind,' says Marcia. 'Well, I'm off to the temple of free speech.' She's glad he's going to picket. It means he's not too old for it, after all. She kisses him again, on the top of his rumpled, sticky head. 'See you for dinner. What're we having?'

Eric thinks for a moment. 'Turnips,' he says.

'Oh good,' says Marcia. 'We haven't had those for a while.'

Marcia puts on her cardigan and her heavy black wool winter coat – not fur, Eric is against fur these days, although Marcia has pointed out that fur is the native way of life and is also biodegradable. She barely gets away with the sheepskin slippers: luckily, their vibrant colour makes them look fake. She adds her boots, her scarf, her lined gloves, and her white wool hat. Thus padded, she takes a breath, clenches all her flesh together, and heads through the door, into the winter. The cat shoots out between her legs and immediately thinks better of it. Marcia lets it back in.

This is the coldest December in a hundred years. At night it hits thirty below; car tires are square in the morning, frostbite cases crowd the hospitals. Eric says it's the greenhouse effect. Marcia is puzzled by this: she thought the greenhouse effect was supposed to make it warmer, not colder. 'Freak weather,' Eric says tersely.

There's ice all over the steps; there has been for days. Marcia has suggested that the mailman may slip on it and sue them, but Eric refuses to use salt: he's in pursuit of some new product that Canadian Tire never seems to have in stock. Marcia holds on to the railing and takes tiny steps downward and wonders if she's getting osteoporosis. She could fall; she could shatter like a dropped plate, like an egg. These are the sorts of possibilities that never occur to Eric. Only large catastrophes concern him.

The sidewalk has been chiselled free of ice, or at least a sort of trail has been made in it, suitable for single file. Marcia makes her way along this, towards the subway station. When she comes out onto Bloor Street it's less treacherous underfoot, but gustier. She breaks into a slow, lumbering trot and reaches the Bathurst station wheezing.

Three of the city's homeless are staked out inside the door. All are young men; two of them are Native Indians, one isn't. The one that isn't puts the twist on Marcia for some change. He says he just wants to eat, which seems to Marcia a modest enough wish: she knows a lot of people who want a good deal more. He is pallid and stubble-faced, and he doesn't meet her eyes. To him she's just a sort of broken pay phone, the kind you can shake to make extra quarters come out.

The two Indians watch without much expression. They look fed up. They've had it with this city, they've had it with suicide as an option, they've had it with the twentieth century. Or so Marcia supposes. She doesn't blame them: the twentieth century has not been a raving success.

At the newsstand she buys a chocolate bar and a *True Woman* magazine, the first Canadian-made but bad for you, the second an outright Yankeeland betrayal. But she's entitled: she gets enough virtuous eating and reality principle in the rest of her life, so for half an hour she'll play hooky and wreck her blood sugar and read escapist trash. She squashes onto the train with the other wool-swaddled passengers and is adroit enough to get a seat, where she thumbs through the holiday fashions and the diet of the month, licking chocolate from her fingers. Then she settles into a piece entitled, with misplaced assurance, 'What Men Really Think.' It's all about sex, of course. Marcia has news for them: the sum total of what men really think is quite a lot bigger than that.

She changes trains, gets off at Union, slogs up the stairs to street level. There's an escalator, but looking at all those slender bodies has made her worried. Eric thinks she has nice thighs; but then Eric leads a sheltered life.

There are underground mazes downtown, underground shopping malls, underground tunnels that can get you from one building to another. You could spend the whole winter underground, without ever going outside. But Marcia feels a moral obligation to deal with winter instead of merely avoiding it. Also, she has a lot of difficulty locating herself on the 'You Are Here' diagrams placed at intervals to help out those lacking in orientation skills. She prefers to be aboveground, where there are street signs.

Just recently she got thoroughly lost down there; the only good thing that happened was that she discovered a store called The Tacki Shoppe, which sold pink flamingo eggs and joke books about sex in middle age, and bottles of sugar pills labelled Screwital. It also sold small pieces of the Berlin Wall, each in its own little box, with a certificate of authenticity included. They cost $12.95. She bought a piece to put in Eric's stocking: they still keep up the habit of jokes in their stockings, from when the children were younger. She is not sure Eric will find this gift funny; more likely, he will make some remark about the trivialization of history. But the children will be interested. The truth is that Marcia secretly wants this piece of the Wall for herself. It's a souvenir for her, not of a place – she has never been to Berlin – but of a time. *This is from the Christmas the Wall came tumbling down*, she will say in later years; to her grandchildren, she hopes. Then she will try to remember what year it was.

More and more, she is squirrelling away bits of time – a photo here, a letter there; she wishes she had saved more of the children's baby clothes, more of their toys. Last month, when Eric took an old shirt that dated from their first year together and cut it up for dishcloths, she saved the buttons. No doubt, after the Berlin Wall fragment has been fingered and exclaimed on Christmas morning, it will end up in this magpie cache of hers.

The wind is worse here, funnelling between the glassy high-rise office buildings. After a block of walking into it, bent over and holding her ears, Marcia takes a taxi.

The paper Marcia writes for is housed in a bland, square, glass-walled, windowless building, put up at some time in the seventies, when airlessness was all the rage. Despite its uninformative exterior, Marcia finds this building sinister, but that may be because she knows what goes on inside it.

The paper is called, somewhat grandiosely, *The World*. It is a national institution of sorts, and, like many other national institutions these days, it is falling apart. Eric says that *The World* has aided the national disintegration in other areas, such as Free Trade, so why should it be exempt itself? Marcia says that, even so, it is a shame. *The World* stood for something once, or so she likes to believe. It had integrity, or at least more integrity than it does now. You could trust it to have principles, to attempt fairness. Now the best you can say of it is that it has a fine tradition behind it, and has seen better days.

Better in some ways, worse in others. For instance, by cutting its staff and tailoring itself for the business community, it is now making more money. It has recently been placed under new management, which includes the editor, a man called Ian

Emmiry. Ian Emmiry was promoted suddenly, over the heads of his elders and seniors, while the unsuspecting former editor was on vacation. This event was staged like a military coup in one of the hotter, seedier nations. It was almost like having a chauffeur promoted to general as the result of some hidden affiliation or pay-off, and has been resented as much.

The journalists who have been there a long time refer to Ian Emmiry as Ian the Terrible, but not in front of the incoming bunch: Ian the Terrible has his spies. There are fewer and fewer of the older journalists and more and more of the newer ones, hand-picked by Ian for their ability to nod. A slow transformation is going on, a slow purge. Even the comic strips at the back have been gutted: for instance, 'Rex Morgan, MD,' with its wooden-faced doctor and its impossibly cheerful and sexless nurse, is no longer to be found. Marcia misses it. It was such a soothing way to start the day, because nothing in it ever changed. It was an antidote to news.

Marcia wanders through the newsroom in search of a free computer. There are no more typewriters, no more clatter, not much of the casual hanging around, the loitering and chit-chat that Marcia links with the old sound of the news being pounded out, drilled out as if from rock. Everything is computers now: Ian the Terrible has seen to that. He is big on systems. The journalists, the new breed, are crouched in front of their computers at their open-plan desks, cooking up the news; they look like pieceworkers in a garment factory.

Marcia does not have her own desk here, because she's not on staff: she's a columnist on contract. So, as Ian said (placing a well-kept hand on her shoulder, his eyes like little zinc nails), she might as well work at home. He would like her to have a computer there, where she would be safely quarantined; he would like her to beam in her columns by modem. Barring that, he would like her to drop her copy off and have it keyboarded into the system by someone else. He suspects her of seditious tendencies. But Marcia has assured him, smiling, that Eric will not allow a computer in the house – he's such a Luddite, but what can you do! – and that she would never expect anyone else to deal with her messy copy. Who could read her handwritten alterations? she has said, diffidently. No, she really has to type the column into the system herself, she tells Ian. She does not say 'keyboard,' and Ian notices this hold-out. Maybe he grits his teeth. It's hard to tell: he has the kind of teeth that appear to be permanently gritted.

Marcia could have a computer at home if she liked. Also, she could bring in clean copy. But she wants to come down here. She wants to see what's going on. She wants the gossip.

Marcia's column appears in the section of the paper that still calls itself 'Lifestyles,' although surely it will have to think up some new heading soon. 'Lifestyles' was the eighties; the nineties are coming, and already steps are being taken to differentiate the decades. Summings-up clutter the papers, radio and television are droning earnestly on about what the eighties meant and what the nineties will mean. People are already talking about the seventies revival, which puzzles Marcia. What is there to revive? The seventies were the sixties until they became the eighties. There were no seventies, really. Or maybe she missed out on them, because that was when the children were small.

Her column, which is read by some men as well as by many women, is about issues. Social issues, problems that may come up: caring for the aged at home, breast-feeding in public, bulimia in the workplace. She interviews people, she writes from the particular to the general; she believes, in what she considers to be an old-fashioned, romantic way, that life is something that happens to individuals, despite the current emphasis on statistics and trends. Lately things have taken a grimmer turn in Marcia's column: there's been more about such things as malnutrition in kindergartens, wife-beating, over-crowding in prisons, child abuse. How to behave if you have a friend with AIDS. Homeless people who ask for hand-outs at the entrances to subway stations.

Ian does not like this new slant of Marcia's; he doesn't like her bad news. Businessmen don't want to read about this stuff, about people who can't work the system. Or so Ian says. She's heard this through the grapevine. He has called her style 'hysterical.' He thinks she's too soppy. Probably she is too soppy. Her days at *The World* are probably numbered.

As she opens a new file on the computer, Ian himself appears. He has on a new suit, a grey one. He looks laminated.

'We got some mail on that column of yours,' he says. 'The one about free needles for junkies.'

'Oh,' says Marcia. 'Hate mail?'

'Most of it,' says Ian. He's pleased by this. 'A lot of people don't think taxpayers' money should be spent on drugs.'

'It's not *drugs*,' says Marcia irritably, 'it's public health.' Even to herself she sounds like a child talking back. In Ian's mind another little black mark has just gone on her chart. Up yours, she thinks, smiling brightly. One of these days she'll say something like that out loud, and then there will be trouble.

Marcia wonders what will happen if she gets fired. Something else may turn up for her; then again, she's getting older, and it may not. She might have to freelance again, or, worse, ghost-write. Usually it's politicians who want the stories of their lives graven in stone for the benefit of future ages, or at least these are the ones who are willing to pay. She did that sort of thing when she was younger and more desperate, before she got the column, but she isn't sure she has the stamina for it any more. She's bitten her tongue enough for one lifetime. She isn't sure she still has the knack of lying.

Luckily, she and Eric have the mortgage on their house almost paid off, and the children are within a few years of finishing university. Eric makes some money on his own, of course. He writes engorged and thunderous books of popular history, about things like the fur trade and the War of 1812, in which he denounces almost everybody. His former colleagues, the academic historians, cross the street to avoid him, partly because they may remember the faculty meetings and conferences at which he also denounced everybody, before he resigned, but partly because they disapprove of him. He does not partake of their measured vocabularies. His books sell well, much better than theirs, and they find that annoying.

But, even with the royalties from Eric's books, there will not be enough money. Also, Eric is slowing down. It has come to him lately that these books have not changed the course of history, and he is running out of steam. Even his denunciations, even his pranks, are rooted in a growing despair. His despair is not focused on any one thing; it's general, like the increasingly bad city air. He doesn't say much about it, but Marcia knows it's there. Every day she fights against it, and breathes it in.

Sometimes he talks about moving – to some other country, somewhere with more self-respect, or somewhere warmer. Or just somewhere else. But where? And how could they afford it?

Marcia will have to bestir herself. She will have to cut corners. She will have to beg – in some way, somehow. She will have to compromise.

Marcia has almost finished typing her column into the computer when her friend Gus drifts by. He says hello to attract her attention, raises his hand in a glass-lifting motion, signals her with a finger: one o'clock. It's an invitation to lunch, and Marcia nods. This charade goes with their shared, only half-humorous pretence that the walls have ears and that it's dangerous for them to be seen too openly together.

The restaurant, their usual, is a Spanish one, well above Bloor Street and far away from *The World* so that they don't expect to run into anyone from there. They arrive at it separately, Marcia first; Gus makes an entrance for her with his coat collar turned up, pausing in the doorway to do a furtive skulk. 'I don't think I was followed,' he says.

'Ian has his methods,' says Marcia. 'Maybe he's a Mountie in disguise. Or CIA, I wouldn't put it past him. Or maybe he's subverted the staff here. He used to be a waiter.' This is untrue, but it's part of an ongoing series of theirs: the former jobs of Ian. (Washroom attendant. Numismatist. Gerbil breeder.)

'No!' says Gus. 'So that's where he got his unctuous charm! Well, that's where I got mine. I did six months of it – in Soho, no less – back when I was a beardless youth. Never be rude to a waiter, darling. They'll spit on your steak in the kitchen.'

Marcia orders a sangria, and settles her widening bottom thankfully into her chair. Here she can eat imported food without feeling like a traitor. She intends to order blood oranges if she can get them. Those, and garlic soup. If Eric cross-examines her later, her conscience will be clear.

Gus is Marcia's latest buddy, and mole, at the paper. Her latest and her last: the others have all been fired or have left. Gus himself is not one of the old guard. He was imported only a few months ago to edit the Entertainment section, in one more of Ian the Terrible's attempts to shore up the credibility of his eroding paper. Even Ian knows there's something wrong, but he's failed to make the connections: he's failed to realize that even businessmen have other interests, and also standards. They've figured out that you can no longer read *The World* to find out what's going on, only to find out what's going on inside Ian's head.

He made a mistake with Gus, though. Gus has his own ideas.

Gus is tall and barrel-shaped and has dark, curly hair. He might be in his mid-thirties, or even younger. He has square, white, even teeth, the same size all the way along, like Mr Punch. This gives him a formidable grin. He is English and Jewish, both at once. To Marcia he seems more English; still, she isn't sure whether his full name is Augustus or Gustav or something else entirely. Possibly he is also gay: it's hard for her to tell with literate Englishmen. Some days they all seem gay to her, other days they all seem not gay. Flirtation is no clue, because Englishmen of this class will flirt with anything. She's noticed this before. They will flirt with dogs if nothing else is handy. What they want is a reaction: they want their charm to have an effect, to be reflected back to them.

Gus flirts with Marcia, lightly and effortlessly, almost as if it were piano practice; or that's what Marcia thinks. She has no intention of taking him seriously and making a fool of herself. Anyway, he's too young. It's only in magazines like *True Woman* that younger men take a severe erotic interest in older women without making invidious comparisons involving body parts. Marcia prefers her dignity, or she intends to prefer it if offered the choice.

Today Gus's flirtation takes the form of an exaggerated interest in Eric, whom he has never met. He wants to know all about Eric. He's found out that Eric's nickname at the paper is Eric the Red, and asks Marcia with false innocence if this has anything to do with Vikings. Marcia finds herself explaining that it's just the way *The World* people think: they think anyone who doesn't agree with them is a communist. Eric is not a communist; instead he's a sort of Tory, but not the kind they have in England. Not even the kind they have now in Canada: Eric thinks the Canadian Tory government is made up mostly of used-car salemen on the make. He is outraged by the Prime Minister's two hundred new suits, not because there are two hundred of them but because they were ordered in Hong Kong. He thinks the taxpayers' money should go to local tailors.

Gus quirks an eyebrow, and Marcia realizes that this conversation is becoming too complicated. As a sort of joke, she says that Gus will never be able to understand Eric unless he studies the War of 1812. That is a war Gus clearly does not remember. He gets out of it by saying that he used to think 'interesting Canadian' was an oxymoron, but that Eric is obviously an exception; and Marcia sees that what he is in search of is eccentricity, and that he has made the mistake of deciding that this is where Eric fits in. She is annoyed, and smiles and orders another drink to keep from showing it. Eric is not so eccentric. About a lot of things he's even right. This doesn't always make him less maddening, but Marcia does not like having him patronized.

Now Gus turns the full force of his attention onto Marcia herself. How does she manage monogamy? he wants to know.

Monogamy is something Marcia and Eric have a reputation for, as others have a reputation for heavy drinking. Monogamy, Gus implies, is a curious anthropological artefact, or else a sort of heroic feat. 'How do you do it?' he asks.

No, Marcia thinks, he is not gay. 'I wasn't always monogamous,' she wants to say. She did not get from one marriage to another along a tidy route. She got there by bad judgements, escapades, misery; Eric himself began as a tumultuous and improbable scuffle. But if she confesses to any of this Gus will only become nosy, or – worse – sceptical, and beg her to tell all. Then, when she does, he'll assume the polite, beady-eyed expression the English get when they think you're too quaint for words, or else boring as hell.

So Marcia avoids the subject, and entertains Gus in other ways. She trots out for him the story of the panties embroidered with the days of the week, and her mother's warnings about being run over by a bus. From there she goes on to construct for him the Canada of old; she describes the dark and dingy Toronto beer parlours with their evil-smelling Men Only sections, she describes the Sunday blue laws. Marcia isn't sure why she wants to make her country out as such a dour and Gothic place. Possibly she wants war stories, like other people. Possibly she wants to appear brave or stalwart, to have endured the rigours of citizenship in such a country. She is suspicious of her own motives.

She tells on, however. She describes Mackenzie King, the longest-ruling Canadian Prime Minister, deciding state policy with the help of his dead mother, who, he was convinced, was inhabiting his pet terrier. Gus thinks she's making this up, but no, she assures him, it's entirely true. There are documents.

This brings them to the end of the garlic soup. When the deep-fried calamari arrive, Gus takes his turn. What he has to offer is gossip about *The World*. 'Ian the Terrible is trying to organize us into pods,' he says. He looks delighted: he has something to add to the list of local adsurdities he is compiling, for when he returns to England. He doesn't know yet that he will return, but Marcia knows. Canada will never be a real place for him.

'Pods?' says Marcia.

'As in killer whales,' says Gus. 'Three writers to a pod, with a pod leader. He thinks it will promote team spirit.'

'He might as well write the whole paper all by himself,' says Marcia, trying not to sound bitter. She thinks the pod idea is extremely stupid, but at the same time she is feeling left out, because she herself has not been included in a pod. She will miss out on something, some of the fun.

'He's working on it,' says Gus. 'He's cut back on the Letters to the Editor to make space for a new column, written by guess who?'

'No,' says Marcia with dismay. 'Called what?'

'"My Opinionzzzz,"' says Gus, grinning his alarming grin. 'No. I lie. "The Snorey of My Life," by Ian Emmiry.'

'You're cruel,' Marcia murmurs, trying to disguise her approval.

'Well, he deserves it. The man should be hanged for the wilful infliction of grievous terminal boredom. He wants the Entertainment section to put on a bun-fest called The Critical Forum. He thinks we should all come in on free overtime to listen to some mouldy old university professor rabbit on about how to keep from going stale. This is not a fabrication.'

'My God,' says Marcia. 'What'll you do?'

'I'm egging him on,' says Gus. 'I smile, and smile, and am a villain.'

'They won't stand for it,' says Marcia.

'That's the general idea,' says Gus, grinning from ear to ear. He's mobile. He does not have a mortgage, or children, or monogamy.

Marcia has downed her second drink too quickly. Now she has lost the thread. Instead of listening, she is staring at Gus, imagining what it would in fact be like to have an affair with him. Too many witticisms, she thinks. Also, he would tell.

She looks at him, shining as he is with naughty pleasure, and all of a sudden she sees what he would have been like as a small boy. A ten-year-old. With that grin, he would have been the class joker. Nobody would have got the better of him, not even the bullies. He'd have known everyone's weak place, where to get the knife in. How to protect himself.

She often thinks this way about men, especially after a drink or two. She can just look at a face and see in past the surface, to that other – child's – face which is still there. She has seen Eric in this way, stocky and freckled and defiant, outraged by schoolyard lapses from honour. She has even seen Ian the Terrible, a stolid, plodding boy who must have known others thought of him as dull; she has seen him studying hard, hoping in vain for a best friend, storing up his revenges. It has helped her to forgive him, somewhat.

Marcia returns to the conversation. She seems to have missed several paragraphs: now Gus has switched focus and is talking about Noriega. 'He's hiding out in the jungle,' he says. 'He's thumbing his nose at them. They'll never get him – he'll be off to Cuba or somewhere – and then it'll just be back to the old graft and squalor, with a brand-new CIA flunkey.' He lifts his glass, signals for a refill. He's drinking white wine. 'A year from now it'll all be fish-wrap.'

Marcia thinks about Noriega, crouching in some tropical thicket or camped out in the hills. She remembers the newspaper photos of him, the round, ravaged, frozen-looking face, the face of a dogged scapegoat. When he was a child it would have been much the same. He would had had those blanked-out eyes very early; they would have been inflicted on him. This is what makes her a soppy columnist, she thinks – she does not believe that children are born evil. She is always too ready to explain.

Marcia goes to the washroom to deal with her overload of sangrias, and to redo her face. It is far later than she has thought. In the mirror she is shiny-eyed, with flushed cheeks; her hair flies out in dishevelled tendrils. From the side – she can just see, rolling her eyes – she has the makings of a double chin. Her first husband used to tell her she looked like a Modigliani; now she resembles a painting from a different age. A plump bacchante of the eighteenth century. She even looks a little dangerous. She realizes with some alarm that Gus is not out of the question, because she herself is not. Not yet.

Marcia force-marches herself up the stairs of the Bathurst station. For a moment she pictures what these squeaky-clean tiled tunnels would be like overgrown with moss or festooned with giant ferns; or underwater, when the greenhouse effect really gets going. She notices she is no longer thinking in terms of *if* – only of *when*. She must watch this tendency to give up, she must get herself under control.

By now it's after five; the three homeless men are gone. Maybe they will be there tomorrow; maybe she will talk with them and write a column about life on the street or the plight of Native people in the city. If she does, it will change little, either for them or for her. They will get a panel discussion, she will get hate mail. She used to think she had some kind of power.

It's dark and cold, the wind whistles past her; in the storefronts the Christmas decorations twinkle falsely. Mostly these are bells and tinsel; the angels and Madonnas and the babes in mangers have been downplayed as being not sufficiently universal. Or maybe they just don't sell things. They don't move the goods.

Marcia hurries north, not dawdling to look. Her bladder is bursting; it doesn't function the way it did; she shouldn't have had that last cup of coffee; she will disgrace herself on the street, like a child in a soggy-bottomed snowsuit, caught out on the way home from school.

When she reaches the house she finds the front steps thoughtfully strewn with kitty litter. Eric has been at work. This becomes more apparent when she rushes to the bathroom, only to find that the toilet paper has been removed. It's been replaced with a stack of newsprint oblongs, which she finds – once she is gratefully sitting and at last able to read – to consist of this morning's *World* business section, neatly scissored.

Eric is in the kitchen, humming to himself as he mashes the turnips. He did away with paper towels some time ago. He wears a white chef's apron, on which to wipe his hands. Earlier dinners have left their tracks; already from tonight's there are several cheerful smears of orange turnip.

The radio news is on: there is more fighting in Panama, there are more dead bodies, there is more rubble, and more homeless children wandering around in it; there are more platitudes. Conspiracy theories are blooming like roses. President Noriega is nowhere to be found, although much is being made of the voodoo paraphernalia and the porn videos that are said to litter his former headquarters. Marcia, having ghost-written the lives of other politicians, does not find any of these details remarkable. Certainly not the porn. As for the voodoo, if that's what it would take to win, most of them would use it like a shot.

'Eric,' she says. 'That cut-up newspaper in the bathroom is going too far.'

Eric gives her a stubborn look; stubborn, and also pleased. 'If they won't recycle at one end, they'll have to be recycled at the other,' he says.

'That stuff will clog the toilet,' says Marcia. An appeal based on poisonous inks absorbed through the nether skin, she knows, will not move him one jot.

'The pioneers did it,' says Eric. 'There was always a mail-order catalogue, on farms. There was never toilet paper.'

'That was different,' says Marcia patiently. 'They had outhouses. You just like the thought of wiping your bum on all those company presidents.'

Eric looks sly; he looks caught out. 'Anything new in the tar pits?' he says, changing the subject.

'Nope,' Marcia says. 'More of the same. Actually it's sort of like the Kremlin down there. The Kremlin in the fifties,' she amends, in view of recent ideological renovations. 'Ian the

Terrible is making them work in pods.'

'As in whales?' says Eric.

'As in peas,' says Marcia. She sits down at the kitchen table, rests her elbows on it. She will not push him on the toilet-paper issue. She'll let him enjoy himself for a few days, or until the first overflow. Then she will simply change things back.

Along with the turnips they're having baked potatoes, and also meat loaf. Eric still allows meat; he doesn't even apologize for it. He says men need it for their red corpuscles; they need it more than women do. Marcia could say something about that, but does not wish to mention such blood-consuming bodily functions as menstruation and childbirth at the dinner table, so she refrains. She also says nothing about having lunch with Gus: she knows that Eric considers Gus – sight unseen, judged only by his feature pieces, which are mostly about Hollywood films – to be trivial and supercilious, and would think worse of her for eating deep-fried calamari with him, especially while Eric himself had been selflessly picketing the US Consulate.

She will not ask Eric about his expedition, not yet. She can tell from his industriousness with the turnips that it has not gone well. Maybe nobody else showed up. There is a candle on the table, there are wineglasses. An attempt at salvaging what is left of the day.

The meat loaf smells wonderful. Marcia says so, and Eric turns off the radio and lights the candle and pours the wine, and gives her a single, beatific smile. It's a smile of acknowledgement, and also of forgiveness – forgiveness for what, Marcia could hardly say. For being as old as she is, for knowing too much. These are their mutual crimes.

Marcia smiles, too, and eats and drinks, and is happy, and outside the kitchen window the wind blows and the world shifts and crumbles and rearranges itself, and time goes on.

What happens to this day? It goes where other days have gone, and will go. Even as she sits here at the kitchen table, eating her applesauce, which is (according to the *Ontario Wintertime*

Cookbook) identical to the applesauce the pioneers ate, Marcia knows that the day itself is seeping away from her, that it will go and will continue to go, and will never come back. Tomorrow the children will arrive, one from the east, one from the west, where they attend their respective universities, being educated in distance. The ice on their winter boots will melt and puddle inside the front door, leaving salt stains on the tiles, and there will be heavy footsteps on the cellar stairs as they descend to do their laundry. There will be rummagings in the refrigerator, crashes as things are dropped; there will be bustle and excitement, real and feigned. The daughter will attempt to organize Marcia's wardrobe and correct her posture, the son will be gallant and awkward and patronizing; both will avoid being hugged too closely, or too long.

The old decorations will be dragged out and the tree will be put up, not without an argument about whether or not a plastic one would be more virtuous. A star will go on top. On Christmas Eve they will all drink some of Eric's killer eggnog and peel the oranges sent by Marcia's first husband. They will play carols on the radio and open one present each, and the children will be restless because they will think they are too old for this, and Eric will take wasteful Polaroids that will never make their way into the albums they always mean to keep up to date, and Noriega will seek asylum at the Vatican Embassy in Panama City. Marcia will learn about this from the news, and from the pages of the contraband *World* that Eric will smuggle into the house and shred later for emergency kitty litter – having used up the real thing on the front steps – and the cat will reject it, choosing instead one of Marcia's invitingly soft pink sheepskin slippers.

Then Christmas Day will come. It will be a Monday, yet another Monday, pastel blue, and they will eat a turkey and some more root vegetables and a mince pie that Marcia will have finally got around to making, while Noriega sleeps unmothered in a room in a house ringed with soldiers, dreaming of how he got there or of how he will get out, or dreaming of nothing, his round face pocked and bleak as an asteroid. The piece of the Berlin Wall that Marcia has given Eric in his stocking will get lost under the chesterfield. The cat will hide.

Marcia will get a little drunk on the eggnog, and later, after the dishes are done, she will cry silently to herself, shut into the bathroom and hugging in her festive arms the grumbling cat, which she will have dragged out from under a bed for this purpose. She will cry because the children are no longer children, or because she herself is not a child any more, or because she can't have a child any more, ever again. Her body has gone past too quickly for her; she has not made herself ready.

It's all this talk of babies, at Christmas. It's all this hope. She gets distracted by it, and has trouble paying attention to the real news.

From *Wilderness Tips*, published by Bloomsbury and Virago.

ice castle

BECKY BIRTHA

I

Gail. Gail Fairchild Jenner. The same Jenner as the city councilman for the West Side. The same Fairchild that the library up on the campus was named for. White Anglo-Saxon Protestants. The Bourgeoisie. What the hell was she doing in love with somebody with a name like that?

Only Maurie didn't know those things at first. She met Gail up on the campus, at the Women's Center, and thought she was just anybody. Somebody going to school part-time at night, somebody halfway poor – just anybody.

Maurie was not a student any more. She'd been out of college a year now. Before that, working the whole time, it had taken her seven years from start to finish. She figured Gail's life might be something like her own.

Gail wore big round glasses. Her large hands kept pushing the short, light brown curls back away from her high forehead, and the curls kept falling back to cover it anyway. Gail was tall and long-limbed, in the standard blue jeans everyone wore but Maurie – who was always coming from work – and an Aran knit sweater Maurie should have known was expensive, only she was thinking Gail would have made it herself. So there was nothing, really, to give Gail Fairchild Jenner away.

'My name's Gail – Gay.' Could she really be that obvious – or that naive? Gay – was she? Was that the point? Now she was laughing, and Maurie was confused. I won't call her that. I'll call her Gail.

And what else had Gail said? Maurie strained to recall every word. It was at the Women's Center's annual poetry reading, and Maurie had been the last to read.

She loved giving readings – that was the one time when she felt completely visible. For all her colorfulness, for all her beads and bangles and bright batik prints, most of the time she felt that other people didn't see all of her. They saw only what mattered most to them at the time – her race, or her gender, or perhaps her age – and then didn't bother to look any further. It was only when she was on stage, standing up among a room full of attentive listeners, that she felt all her colors leap into focus.

Here in this wintry city, surrounded by pale, restrained faces, her full-blown features and deep colors felt like a rich, tropical ripeness. Her tan skin, freshly oiled, held the faint smell of coconut and glowed beneath the sliding silver bracelets that rang against one another when she lifted her hands. She could feel the same glow in her face. The trade beads and cowrie shells that she had braided into her hair swung and clattered softly against one another. And the soft lamplight picked up all the colors in the woven fabric she wore around her shoulders – the saffron yellow, the green, the earth red and the black. At times like this she felt thoroughly visible and utterly sure of herself, high and happy and perfectly loveable.

She loved reading last because she felt like the spotlight stayed on her, a lingering aura, long after the program was over. Her words would be the ones that echoed in people's memories; she would be the one they came up to talk to over the wine and cheese. And maybe some night some new person would come, excited by her work, curious about her life...

She balanced her Wheat Thins and mozzarella cheese in a napkin and turned around to find Gail standing before her, long-legged and spare in the loose, bone-colored sweater, a spill of tousled brown curls capping her face.

'You're good,' was the first thing Gail said.

'Thanks,' Maurie said, smiling, pleased. And Gail was smiling back, her gray-blue eyes keeping Maurie's with an intensity that held her connected, in spite of the chattering crowd. So that Maurie waited, knowing they had more to say to each other.

'Why do you write poetry?'

It was a question nobody had ever asked after a reading, and it took her so unexpectedly that Maurie told the truth without thinking. 'Because I want people to love me.'

Gail let out a gasp of surprised laughter. 'Seriously? Does it work? Do they?'

'I don't know...' Maurie was suddenly self-conscious. 'They don't tell...'

'No one has ever walked up to you after a reading and said, "Hey."' And for a moment everything stopped and hung, precarious. '"I've fallen in love with you."'

Maurie stared, caught in the storm-colored eyes. Gail stood so close that Maurie could inhale the faint, warm scent of her skin, damp beneath the layers of jersey and wool. She was still smiling, but now the line of her smile was a question, waiting.

How did we start talking about this? Who *is* this woman, and why is she asking me this?

'I didn't mean I'd expect somebody to do that.' She was losing ground, the performer's sureness and self-confidence ebbing away. She turned back to the refreshment table, and Gail was right beside her, filling Maurie's Dixie cup from the half-gallon jug of wine, and then filling her own.

'But you'd like it if someone did.' Her voice was too low, too familiar, and Maurie backed up a step. What was going on? Was Gail coming on to her? Was this how women...got started? She was confused, nonplussed, yet at the same time still pleased.

'Well, everybody wants to be loved.' But what she was thinking was that all the poems she had read that night had been about women. She had planned it that way as a matter of course, because this was the Women's Center. But all those women in the poems. So what must this Gail think? Maurie took a swallow, the purple liquor sharp in her throat.

'And you…fall in love with people very easily.'

No one ever talked to her this way. Gail's words, the closeness of her seemed to demand an answer. Her expectant eyes were like a wide, wet winter sky. 'Yes,' Maurie admitted. 'Yes, I fall in love with people all the time.'

'Maurie, hi. I really like that one poem you read – about the old woman in the bandana, on the bus, and how she used to be the prettiest girl at all the dances…' She was aware of the event again, the festivity. That whole business with Gail had scarcely taken a minute. No one had even left yet. But now Roberta was asking her, 'Do you want a ride? I have to leave now, because I promised Gary I'd pick him up after his class.'

'I don't think I'm ready to leave yet. But thanks, anyway.' She said it with no idea how she would get back to the West Side. Of course, she could take the bus, but they ran so seldom after nine at night. She pictured the dark, deserted corner where she'd have to get off the Main Street bus and wait for the Twenty-six. There was nothing there – just the tall iron fence and wide gates of the cemetery behind her, and the flick of car lights cruising across her body, one after another. She knew it wasn't safe. She didn't care.

There was the rest of the social thing spinning out. She talked to the other readers, to women she remembered from her English classes. She drank Chianti in the Dixie cup and listened, asked questions and answered questions, and watched Gail across the room, drinking Chianti, too, but standing alone. It was plain Gail was watching her, was waiting, too, for this to be over.

The crowd gradually thinned, quieted, until the last women

had their coats on, at the door, and one of them looked from Gail to Maurie and said, 'You two got a way to get home?' *You two.* At the same time they both said yes, and the woman who'd asked them said, 'OK. I need to drop these evaluations off at American Studies, and then I'll be back to lock up. But if your ride comes before that, could you just make sure the door's shut tight?'

'*Do* we have a ride home?' Maurie asked, after the others were gone.

Gail nodded, added, 'We might have to wait awhile. My sister's supposed to pick me up.' Gail dropped down on the couch at the side of the room and stretched out. Maurie hesitated, then sat down crosslegged on the floor near the end of the couch. She leaned against the wall. The room that had been crowded too small a few minutes before was suddenly vast and silent. She couldn't take her eyes off Gail's curly head, lying on her sweater-clad arms…

'Maurie.' It was the first time Gail said her name. 'Maurie, do you ever fall in love with women?'

'Oh, yeah. At least as often as I've fallen in love with men.' That muddled everything. Why had she brought up men? She wasn't being clear. But it wasn't clear, anymore, even to her. She *had* fallen in love with men. And women, too. She would try to tell what was true. 'I've fallen in love with women lots of times. But nothing's ever come of it. We never did anything about it. Or maybe they didn't feel the same way…'

She'd often imagined it otherwise – the woman with whom things would go differently. A woman her age, or maybe a little older, with the same experiences behind her. Who'd already been through college, and communes, and consciousness-raising groups, and was through with all the double dealing and disappointments that went down with men. Who was just as ready, now, as she.

'Maurie, how old are you?'

'Twenty-five.'

Gail sat up on the couch and drew her kees in suddenly to her chest. 'How old do you think I am?'

'I don't know.' She began to look at Gail closely, at the smooth unblemished complexion, the gangly, still awkward limbs.

'Younger than me,' she said slowly. 'Maybe twenty-one or…twenty.'

'I just turned seventeen last week.'

The sister who came didn't look anything like Gail. The dark fringe of bangs that edged straight across her brow gave her face a scowl. Or maybe that scowl was because of Maurie…In the dark car, in their bulky winter clothing, the three of them sat squeezed together in the front seat while the radio played AM inanity. She could tell when Gail turned toward her, feel her eyes on her. It was too dangerous to turn and meet them; she kept her focus out through the windshield.

There had been no snowfall to speak of yet, this year. The dry, scant flickers that were falling now would not stay on the ground. Still, Gail's sister steered the big station wagon carefully through the deserted streets. In Gail's family, there were still another sister and three brother Jenners. Six altogether. They'd be all over the West Side!

Maurie tried to think of the things to say that the sister might expect from her. But she felt slow, flushed and heavy-headed, too stoned. She wished desperately that she and Gail could be alone. Gail's mittened hand lay against Maurie's corduroy covered thigh – loosely, casually, staying.

II

As much as Maurie hated the winter, hated going out in the cold, three times in three days she walked up toward Chapin Parkway. Her face burned in the assault of the wind; her toes froze after the first five minutes. She walked toward the block of the Parkway where Gail lived – only five blocks from Maurie's apartment – coming closer each time, and then going home. The third time she walked past the house. It was stone, set back

71

in a deep lawn, with a drive curving around the side. It seemed to have hundreds of windows, all of them polished bright and shining like magnifying glasses.

She felt outrageously conspicuous. In her life, among people she didn't know, she often felt exotic. She liked that feeling, to be someone special who stood out from the crowd. But in this neighborhood, even though there was not another person on the block, she felt garish and outlandish. The color of her skin felt like a sunlamp burn – over-exposed and wrong. The beads she had braided into her hair seemed artless, and the colors in her skirt, the bright lacings in her knee-high boots, loud and gaudy. She kept her eyes focused straight ahead, and did not look to see who might be watching from those many windows.

Gail had given her a phone number, but she couldn't call her. Not at home. Among all those people, the odds that Gail would pick up the phone were only one in nine. Who could she tell them she was?

Evenings when she stayed in her apartment, she sat by the window, waiting, watching the sky darkening into that deep, luminous blue – a long half hour. Then indigo. Then night. Outside in the alley, the wind whipped and wheeled, rattling the glass, shrieking and whistling round the corners of the building. She was glad there was still no snow. But without it the winter seemed even more relentless.

Nobody would be out walking on nights like this. She could come. She could bundle up so well that no one would recognize her anyway. And no one would see her turn down the alley, slip in at the downstairs door. Come on Gail. You have to come here. Because I can never come to you. A white woman, a younger woman could maybe get away with it. Show up some Saturday afternoon in Nikes and a baggy sweatshirt, just 'Tell your Mama and your Papa I'm a little schoolgirl, too.' But not Maurie.

Saturday night she turned the radio to the blues show that came on every week. She was drinking vin rose. She might as well keep on, and get drunk by herself. It seemed appropriate. It was late, going on eleven, when the phone rang.

'I couldn't call you before. My brother Ted listens to everyone's phone calls. This family is like the headquarters of the FBI. My kid sister Wendy snoops in my drawers all the time. And my mother's just as bad – always finding excuses to poke around in my room. Daddy just "checks up" – you know, finds out from neighbors and friends of his where you've been seen and in the company of whom. I hate living in this family!'

'Sounds familiar.' Maurie grinned into the receiver. 'I couldn't wait to go away to school.' She'd had to pay a high price for that privilege – waiting tables, typing, through the summers and the semesters, too.

'I wanted to live in the dorm, but they wouldn't let me. They think I'm too young. And anyway, they're not going to pay room and board for me to live at the other end of the same town. Not that they couldn't afford it.'

'Listen,' Maurie broke in. 'Can we…did your brother go out tonight? The one who listens to your calls, I mean.'

'Oh, I'm not at home.'

'Where are you?' She pictured Gail standing in a telephone booth while the traffic passed and the wind stormed at the glass walls. There was a pay phone on the corner of Elmwood Avenue, half a block away. Maybe Gail had forgotten exactly where Maurie lived…

'I'm babysitting tonight. The kids finally went to sleep.'

'Oh. Babysitting.'

'You have a regular job, don't you?' Gail's voice was wistful. 'What do you do?'

'I teach. At a co-op pre-school.' For a second she thought about the children in her class, their parents…What would they think if they knew what she was up to? What *was* she up to? Trying to seduce a seventeen-year-old kid?

'What about you?' she asked. 'What are you doing in school?'

'Failing.' Laughing. Nervous, embarrassed.

'Why?'

'I'm not doing it on purpose. I just – don't care about it enough. It's not that important to me.'

'What is important to you?' Wishing she would say, 'You.'

'I don't know,' Gail said. 'I'm trying to figure that out. I'm real depressed a lot of the time. I drink too much. Sometimes I think I'm suicidal.'

'Maybe you don't belong in school right now. Christ, you only just *turned* seventeen. You must be precocious as hell.'

'But I'm *failing*.'

'That happens to a lot of people,' Maurie said. 'I failed courses my first year in college, too.'

'But I'm supposed to be so spectacular. Everybody's holding their breath, waiting for me to distinguish myself. Since I refuse to be a social butterfly, I'm supposed to be a scholar.'

'They *want* you to be a social butterfly?'

'You don't know my family,' Gail said. 'I mean, my mother sent me to etiquette school. And dancing lessons. Then, last year, I was supposed to be a debutante. We almost came to blows over that.'

Maurie laughed. 'You don't mean that, seriously?'

'Yeah, I do. Some etiquette, huh? She used to hit me all the time when I was little. Just over anything. Like if I left my stuff on the dining room table, or if I forgot to change my clothes when I came home from school. She was always hitting me. Now that I'm bigger than her, she doesn't dare. But she gets her way most of the time, anyway.'

Her own anger flared up so fully and swiftly it surprised Maurie. She could see Gail as, maybe, a ten-year-old: an awkward, big-boned child who could never do anything right – blinking back tears from the red-faced sting of a full-handed slap. Those people. They had everything. Why did they have to hit a kid?

'My mother drinks even more than I do,' Gail said. 'I think she's an alcoholic.'

'What about your father?' Maurie asked, finally.

'Dad's OK, I guess. He's pretty liberal, compared to a lot of kids' parents. He doesn't try to run my life too much. He just doesn't understand – about this college thing – that this just isn't what I want to be doing.'

'And what is it,' she asked again, 'you'd rather be doing?'

Gail was thinking. 'I really love track,' she said, after a little while. 'I guess I'd just spend all my time doing sports if I could. Hey,' her voice suddenly came alive. 'Do you run?'

'No…'

'Do you play tennis? Do you ski?'

Maurie sat holding the phone, wishing, for the first time in years, that she were somebody else.

After she hung up, Maurie thought over what more she knew of Gail now. Not much. Gail played the clarinet. Badly. But her mother didn't want her to quit. Gail had never held down a paying job in her life. Gail definitely did not belong in a ballroom…But why hadn't Maurie asked the things she really wanted to know? Why hadn't she asked Gail if *she* ever fell in love with women? Or when she could see her again?

Gail called her once – twice again. From another sitting job, from the campus one night. No, her mother always expected her home for dinner. She'd want to know who the friend was, to meet her first. She was going on a skiing trip this weekend with her sister's youth group from church. She had exams to study for next week – final exams. It was a joke; she knew she would fail them all. But studying would look good, anyway. Her parents didn't have any idea – and the blow wouldn't fall until they got her grades in January.

'I didn't expect you to be home again on a Saturday night,' she told Maurie. 'Two weeks in a row. Don't you ever go out?'

'I guess I'm not much of a party-goer.' But she had been asked to a party – over at Wendell's tonight. She'd forgotten, conveniently, wanting to stay home in case the phone rang.

'What were you doing?'

Drinking again. Wishing you'd call. Writing a poem about you. 'Nothing.'

The other nights – when Gail didn't call – would lag and creep. This was not the way she had expected this thing to go.

She wasn't sure what exactly she had wanted, but knew this wasn't turning out to be it. Sometimes the tedium sent Maurie out of the house, hurled her into the early darkness to force her way against the wind, up Elmwood Avenue, toward the Parkway. The wind chill factor was often well below zero, but at least it hadn't snowed yet. The shops along the Avenue were open late, lit up for the holidays. Maybe Gail would have to do some Christmas shopping…

Roberta and Gary lived on Elmwood Avenue. She hadn't called or stopped in to visit for a long time. She didn't do it now. What could she say when they asked what was going on in her life?

Wendell lived a few blocks down, on Lafayette. She could imagine his response. He'd pretend that he was trying to take her seriously. 'Now wait a minute. Lemme make sure I get this straight. She rich. She white. And she *how* old? And you in *what* with this chick?' She had always thought Wendell was fun, had always laughed at the way he spared no one, nothing with his jokes. Now she felt like she had to protect herself.

Once, when she got off work at three-thirty, instead of going home she took the bus in the other direction – up to the campus. She wandered around randomly, then bought coffee in the Rathskellar – where students who were failing usually hung out. Sitting alone, drinking her coffee, it occurred to her that the answer was to go away. She would go away for Christmas – back to Boston, to spend the holiday with her family. Maybe it would put this whole thing in a different perspective. Maybe she would forget all about Gail.

III

Then she came. Two days before Maurie was to leave for Boston, the phone rang – nine o'clock on Saturday morning – and she knew in an instant it was Gail. 'Listen. I could come over this morning. My mother's out of town and Nancy and Ted are off in Williamsburg at my cousins'. I have to go to a music lesson this afternoon, but I have a couple of hours until then…'

Gail seemed to take up all the space in Maurie's small, square living room. She sat on the couch – it was a day bed, really – and made the legs look spindly, rickety. She slouched down, and her long legs stretched most of the way across the floor. She had thrown the bright blue jacket on the only other chair, where it collapsed looking winded, with its arms flung out. Now Gail was rubbing the fog from her glasses in the folds of another expensive sweater – soft blue and green. In the daylight, her short curls looked more gold than brown.

'Are you hungry?' Maurie asked. 'I mean, I was just going to fix myself some breakfast when you called. So I thought I'd wait to see if you wanted some too.'

A wide smile. 'What are you having?' An adolescent's insatiable appetite.

'Eggs and toast, and orange juice. I could make you eggs, however you like.'

Gail was interested, had followed her into the narrow kitchen. 'How are you having yours?'

'Poached.'

'I'll have one, too.'

She filled the saucepan and set it on the burner, began to slice the bread. 'One poached egg on toast, coming up.'

'No, just plain.'

'Just plain? Just one egg? All by itself?' Maurie had never eaten a poached egg except on toast, in her whole life. 'You don't want *any* toast?'

'Well, maybe one piece. On the side.'

Her own eggs came out perfect, every morning. This morning she did everything the same way she always did, boiling the water and turning it down, then stirring to make a funnel in the center of the pot, slipping the egg from the saucer into the swirling center. But the white splayed out from the yolk and spread, in lumpy streamers, all through the water. She had forgotten to flip the timer, and as soon as she scooped the egg out, she knew it would be runny and underdone. It sat there, a pale and almost colorless blob, while the water ran off into a puddle around it, on the white china plate. She had forgotten the toast, and now it was scorched from her quirky, antiquated toaster, one side undone, the other crisp black. She forgot to put the salt on the table, too, didn't think of it until she sat down to eat her own egg – and Gail was already finished by then. There was no butter, because Maurie never bought anything but margarine. But Gail insisted that everything was fine.

Maurie had imagined this visit so many times. She had always thought it would be evening – the two of them surrounded by quiet jazz and soft lamplight. She had wanted Gail to be charmed by her tiny apartment, and the way she had decorated it – the brilliant African fabric that covered one wall in a sunburst of color, and the instruments: the big-bellied calabash with its shiny beads that hung from a strap on the wall above the chair, the tall conga drum in the corner. Sometimes when people came in they would start to play with the instruments. Almost no one could resist the kalimba, resist pressing a few notes from its flat metal prongs. And then, later, she'd thought that Gail might ask to see more of her poetry…

But Gail was restless, moving quickly from the kitchen back to the other room, stretching her long legs out, drawing them in, taking off her glasses and cleaning them again, glancing from time to time out the window that faced on the empty alley. 'Let's go out,' she said.

'Out? But…it's freezing. It looks like it's going to snow.'

Gail's eyes were excited, alive for the first time since she'd come. 'Maybe it will!' And when Maurie joined her at the window, kneeling beside her on the couch, Gail said, 'It was beautiful, walking over here. The clouds are so thick, and so low…We can go over to the cemetery. There's never anybody there.'

Never anybody there – to see what? Go to the cemetery – and do what? Go for a *walk*, *in Buffalo*, in *December*? Incredible as it seemed, she was pulling on her own sweater, her jacket, muffler, going out to walk in the cemetery, in the middle of winter, with Gail.

*

They walked side by side, following the wide road that led through the center of the grounds. Everything was frozen solid – the stiff colorless grass and the creek. It seemed as if their voices had frozen up inside them. There was no sound, except the crunch of the two pairs of boots in the gravel at the edge of the road, and now and then a bird calling.

They didn't touch. Yet Maurie could feel a kind of aura, like a magnetic field, surrounding Gail, as though there were electric in the blue of Gail's down jacket, a charged field that was tangibly alive, the closer Maurie's body shifted toward Gail's. She wondered if Gail could feel it, too.

Gail took long steps, her hands swinging at her sides, and stared straight ahead into the distance, at the bare lace of tree branches far off against the low gray sky. Maybe Maurie was wrong. Maybe Gail didn't feel anything. And nothing was going to happen – not today, not any other day. Maybe thinking that there was anything between them was just building castles in the air – fantastic creations spun from nothing – elaborate towers, tunnels and turrets, whimsical twists and turns. Elegant fragile architecture that simply wasn't there.

In the air – but what she pictured was a castle made of ice. High walls arched into vast doorways and cathedral roofs. Down long halls, footsteps rang like bells and echoed up the steep stairways, through the vaulted, empty rooms. Exquisitely beautiful – but not a place where anyone could live, not a place she could stay. The air inside – cold as crushed crystal, filling the lungs. The castle perfect, solid and sound, as shiny and smooth as glass. On the first day of summer it would be gone.

Gail's voice, disappointed, broke the silence. 'It isn't going to snow. It's too cold.' And then, a few steps further, 'I have to head back. I've got to get to my lesson.'

'Gail?' Maurie's own voice sounded as sharp, as penetrating as a bird's. A gulp of cold air slid down her throat. 'Gail, are you a lesbian?'

There was a long, quiet stretch. They were going uphill, and she could hear herself breathing hard, the air coming forth in rhythmic puffs from her open lips. Finally Gail answered.

'I don't know. I've never been – involved with anyone. But I think it would be women – a woman – if I did.'

Maurie didn't think before she said the next words – they just came. 'Are you afraid of me?'

Gail turned to her, surprised. But there was something else – relief – in her face. 'Yeah. You're right. Yeah, I guess I am.'

'Of what? Why?' And when Gail didn't answer, just shook her head, she asked, 'What do you think of me? I mean, who did you think I was? Why did you want to know me?'

Gail turned to her as if to explore Maurie's face for the answer. 'I *did* want to know you. I mean I still do. But it was…you just seemed so different from me. I don't mean just…' she looked away, then back, 'in the obvious ways. Well, maybe that's part of it, but it was more. There's a way you've got about you – standing up there reading those poems, you just seemed so sure of yourself, so absolutely you. All the while you were reading I kept thinking – I saw something in you that I wanted, wanted to have, wanted to be…'

Gail's stride was still long, determined, the heels of her boots biting into the frozen gravel. But the pace had slowed. 'When we gave you a ride home, and I saw where you lived, on that alley over that garage, all by yourself, I just thought you must have your life all together, exactly the way you want it to be. And then I couldn't imagine what you were doing trying to let me into it. I thought – I must have been wrong about you. I thought you'd know better than that.'

'You think that little of yourself?'

More long, silent steps, slower. Gail's head was down now, eyes on the toes of her boots, and she didn't answer.

'So is that what you think of me, now? That I'm not all that wonderful after all, since I want to be…friends with you?'

'I don't know what to think any more.' At the crest of the hill, as Gail raised her head, a draft of wind lifted the muffler at her neck, blew back the loose spray of curls around the edge of her face, and settled it back. They walked on. 'I think, maybe,'

Gail said, 'I'm not sure if I should see you again.'

The words tumbled the world awry. Panic, fear flew flapping through Maurie like a wounded bird. 'You don't want to see me again?'

'Oh, yeah. I'd like to…'

The unspoken end of Gail's sentence hung in the air – the part that began with the word 'but' – while the panic inside Maurie lurched and beat. She asked, 'Because of your family?'

'No, not them.' Gail flicked her head in a single, abrupt shake. 'They can't run my life forever. I just don't want to – ruin it for you.'

'Ruin how? Ruin what?'

'Anything – everything.'

They kept walking, back the way they had come. Beside her, Gail's green woolen mittens swung at her sides, in the rhythm of her stride. Her face was downcast again.

The noise of traffic was audible once more – a long lean on a car horn, and now the loose, futile clanking of somebody's snow chains against the dry road surface. The Delaware Avenue gate loomed suddenly just a few yards away.

Maurie's face, her hands, even her toes were tingling with heat. 'Look,' she said, the words crowding out in a rush. 'You don't have to protect me. Maybe you don't like yourself all that much, but I like you…' In Gail's face she caught her response – the quick flash of irrepressible pleasure. '…And I want to see you again.'

At the corner of Gail's block they stood lingering awkwardly by the curb. As if she could hear the question in Maurie's mind, Gail said, 'I'm going to be out of town for a couple weeks. I have to go to my grandparents' in Philadelphia, and then down to St Croix…'

'St Croix!'

But Gail was shaking her head. 'It's no big deal. We go practically every year. My whole family's going to be there – and believe me, they could ruin Paradise!'

'When will you be back?'

'Saturday before New Year's.'

Someone came out of one of the houses on Gail's block, and they both grew suddenly alert, moved another foot apart – then caught each other's eyes in a sheepish smile. 'I'm going away, too,' Maurie said. 'Down to Boston, to spend Christmas with my folks.'

Gail laughed. 'God, I wish I didn't have to do that. And you're going five hundred miles out of your way so that you can? Incredible!'

Now a car pulled into a drive at the far end of the street, and Gail half turned to go, squinting down the block.

'Will you call me when you get back, Gail?'

'OK.'

'Is that a promise?'

'I don't know…'

IV

The child in the picture wore a crimson dress and carried a lunch pail in one hand and a schoolbag that looked enormous in the other. A complicated pattern of elaborate cornrows framed her penny brown face. Her wide smile was toothless in the front.

'Kasinda. The first day of school.'

'That's right.'

'This is priceless. Would you ask Aunt Laverne to get a copy made for me?'

'You can ask her yourself, Maurie. They'll be over tomorrow night.'

'For dinner? The kids and everyone?'

'Kids and all. Laverne said I'd better not let you sneak out of here this time without her getting a chance to see you. She says the last time she had a good talk with you was that summer we were all down on the Cape at Joe Franklin's place. That was two years ago, if it was a day. Laverne wasn't even expecting Zaki yet.' Maurie's mother moved back to the stove and lifted the lid on the pot roast. The aroma of onions and hot, meaty juices steamed out into the kitchen.

Maurie watched her movements, feeling half at home, and half like a guest. She always expected things in this house to look exactly as they had all the while she was growing up – when there was no money for new appliances and floors. But Pop and Uncle Jerome had redone the kitchen three years ago. And now, here was this modern, avocado-colored, six-burner range – and then on top of it that old blue and white mottled pot with the chipped lid, the one that had been on the stove Sundays and holidays ever since Maurie could remember.

Her mother, too, was a study in contrasts. The gray knit pants and yellow jersey would have looked as fresh and modern as the new kitchen, except for the faded print apron, ruffled and rick-racked, that completed her outfit. Maurie and Toby had given it to her for Mother's Day, some fifteen years ago.

'We ought to do that again. You could get down for a week or two in the summer, couldn't you?'

Yes, she could come back, year after year, and know exactly what to expect. But what if, one year, she didn't come? Or brought somebody with her?

'This ought to be done right on time. I just have to make up a pan of rolls and…'

'I'll do the rolls.' She uncovered the bowl of dough, searched under the sink for the square tin her mother always used. She tried to imagine Gail in this kitchen. Gail wouldn't know which pan to use for the bread, or the melted butter. Would her hands know how to shape rolls? Would she seem to take up all the space in this kitchen the way she had in Maurie's apartment? Would everything here look too gaudy and new, or too shabby and old?

When she cleared the table, she looked again through the pictures. Most of them were of the children – Kasinda and Kalil and their baby brother. There was one of her aunt and uncle together, in wet bathing suits, with their arms around one another. Something that simple. Just a picture of the two of you, at the beach last summer, to send home to the folks...She squared the edges of the stack of photos and dropped them back into their bright yellow envelope. She wiped across the oilcloth with the damp dishrag.

At Christmas dinner the following afternoon, they were all there in person – along with her maternal grandmother, a great aunt and a second cousin. Her brother Toby had driven in from New Haven. Pop did almost all the talking, and still managed to eat most of the rolls. Mom ran in and out of the kitchen and never got around to taking off her apron. When the baby turned his bowl upside down and everyone laughed, Toby made a face at Maurie across the table and, down at the other end, Kasinda made practically the same face at Kalil. Everything going according to plan – everybody doing exactly what was expected.

And what would all the family do if she told them? Or somehow they found out? Looking around the table, she couldn't imagine a setting in which what she was contemplating could be more scandalous. Unless maybe it was *her* parents' house. What was Gail doing now? Were several generations of Jenners sitting down to a formal candlelit Christmas dinner in Philadelphia? Roast goose? Plum pudding? Champagne? Were they having a barbecue on a beach in St Croix? Was Gail thinking about Maurie?

Finally, the next day, she got to sneak away with Toby. They drove into town and then over the bridge across the Charles, into Cambridge, parked the car and walked through the Common toward Harvard Square. Toby pulled his pipe from the wide pocket of his softly padded jacket. The bowl was already filled and ready to light. At home, he never smoked. She wasn't even sure if Mom and Pop knew he smoked a pipe. *She* had never told them.

He inhaled the first breath and blew it out in a blue puff. 'God, it's good to get out of there. That place always makes me feel like I'm ten years old. It's like a time warp, every time I come back.' She nodded and laughed along with him. 'You'd hardly believe I was a fully functioning adult back in New Haven. Whatever Pop wants me to do, I end up going along with it. I can't say no to him any easier than I could when I was only four foot tall.'

She remembered him like that – four foot tall – a skinny kid with a narrow chest who couldn't fight or even insult people properly, who got teased unmercifully for his sallow 'yellow' complexion and his tight black curls, and who cried more easily than she did. Pop had always wanted Toby to learn to fight back...She and Toby had never, either of them, fit in, but they managed to make it all right for each other.

In the summertime, when all the other kids were out playing, both of them carrying books home from the library together made it all right. When he started reading *The Daily Worker* every day, and going to the Du Bois Club meetings after school, she acted like that was perfectly normal behavior for a fifteen-year-old boy. When she wore her beads and peasant skirt and sandals, and a huddle of girls on a porch giggled as she and Toby walked by, and then one of them called out, ' Hey girl! Don't you know they ain't no such thing as black hippies?' Toby pretended he hadn't heard a thing.

He had still been that skinny-chested kid, all through high school, but now – she watched him while he talked. Now his hands were big and competent looking, one of them waving the pipe around to accent his words. Now his chest was broad as a barrel, and his skin had weathered to a richer tone, like fine leather. Now there was a short thick beard, that matched the curls. She hadn't paid much attention to his changing, but today here he was – a grown man.

'Did you see me up on the ladder? Gee, I thought the whole neighborhood was watching. I swear I thought I was gonna break my neck, perched up there with all those strings of lights draped around me. I felt like a blasted Christmas tree. You know where the steps are, at the front of the porch. Well, you can't set the ladder flat because of the steps. Pop's supposed to be holding the ladder steady; instead he's checking out all the extension cords going, "Wait a minute – this ain't the right one here – no – this one don't fit together…" I thought any second he's gonna plug in the wrong one, and I'm gonna light up and go blinking off and on. They can just leave me up here, and forget about Christmas decorations.'

'Remember that time they were going out, and Pop was instructing us about what to do in case the Christmas tree caught on fire?' she asked, laughing.

'Yeah.' Toby mimicked Pop's most serious face, and they both said it, chanting out in unison, just as they had in answer to Pop's question that night long ago. 'Crawl under the Christmas tree and pull out the cord.'

'I woulda done it too,' Toby said, shaking his head. 'I probably would do it today, if Pop told me to.'

'What gets me,' she said, 'is how I feel like I can't talk about what's really going on in my life. Like they don't really want to know that I *have* a life, outside of them. So I feel like I'm only half real.'

'Yeah, I know. Same here.' He looked across at her, from under the Greek fisherman's cap that was pulled down low on one side, his familiar black eyes twinkling, set deep in the tan face. When they were kids, he used to claim he could read her mind. 'So what really is going on in your life? You writing much?'

'Some.' She hoped he wouldn't ask if she'd brought any of her new poems with her this trip. Lately, they were all love poems about Gail. She added, 'Nothing terribly profound.'

When she didn't elaborate, he went on. 'How's your love life? You know – the big "S"?'

She shook her head. 'Nonexistent.' But her face was suddenly hot. Nobody but Toby would have seen the subtle color change.

He looked at her closer, a smile widening his face. 'You fell for somebody, huh? Or somebody fell for you.'

'Cut it out, Toby. I'm entitled to a private life.' Yet she really wanted to tell him. The way she'd been able to tell no one but him when she was twelve and that man in the car had stopped her to ask for directions, and she'd gone up to the window – how frightened she'd been when she saw he had his pants down all the way around his ankles…She wanted to tell the way she'd been able to, years later, when she first had sex with a man, and Toby had reassured her that it was all right, that she didn't have to feel guilty, that passion was a perfectly healthy, moral thing to feel. The way he'd been able to tell her, when he was going out with a white girl – Rochelle Herman – when Maurie and Toby were both still in high school, and he trusted Maurie not to tell their parents, and she never did. And then, in New Haven, when he was living with Aileen. Maurie had gone and stayed with them, and thought of Aileen as a sister-in-law, those two years. But she never told.

'Who's the lucky guy?' he teased.

'It's nothing like that. It's…just a crush. A bad crush – that won't amount to anything.' She could hear Stevie Wonder's voice singing accusingly. 'You got it bad girl…'

'You can tell,' he said again. 'We're all adults here.'

I wish we were. Instead she said, 'Isn't that strange, Toby? Isn't it? We *are* adults, finally – you and me. When I was a kid I used to look at Mom and Uncle Jerome sometimes, and think about how they were sister and brother, Toby, like you and me. And that now they were two grownups – but they were *still* sister and brother. And I couldn't get over that fact. It just used to amaze me. I always wondered what it would feel like, if it ever happened to us. And now here we are – a grown-up sister and brother…'

'Crossing the Common in the chill December air,' he struck a pose, pipe in hand, 'trudging through the dry, decaying leaves, reminiscing about our lost youth…'

'Yeah.' She giggled. 'Walking and talking – just a couple of boring grownups.'

At the end of the day, after another company dinner, after a long evening of her father's stories, and his interminable advice, she sat on the bed in the little room at the back of the second floor. Yellow print curtains she had chosen when she was fourteen still hung at the window. The desk, unbelievably small and impractical, stood in the corner, and on the shelves above it were the few children's books that she had managed to get second hand, after falling in love with copies borrowed from the public library: Laura Ingalls Wilder, Edith Nesbitt, Marguerite Di Angeli. What a strange child she must have been growing up black in Boston, in the 1960s, and reading all the time of prairies and gardens and moors, about children from Sweden and England, writing poems about places she had never seen, and wishing she came from some exotic, faraway land, too – not being able to see who she was.

She remembered, she used to light the room with candles when her parents were not at home. The flickering flames made the colors dance in the psychedelic posters she had taped on the wall. That part had come later. But now it was all mixed up together with the little girl stuff. *Siddhartha* and *The Prophet* sat on the shelf right next to *A Little Princess*. A box of incense lay on the windowsill beside a cluster of china horses – God, her mother must come in here and dust this stuff every week.

She took a stick of incense from the package and lit a match to its end. In a curl of pungent sandalwood smoke, those last years came rushing back. How trapped she had felt in this room, burning incense and candles, how powerless to change anything about her life. It was easy, when she was here, to slide into feeling powerless again. Just like Toby had said...But she hadn't really been powerless, even then. She had left home...

She stood up and faced herself in the mirror that hung over the dresser. It was such a small mirror only her face showed. She hadn't wanted any mirror, in those days. It had taken her so long to learn to love herself, as she was.

But she did now. She studied the face framed in the square of dark wood, and she liked everything she saw – the thick eyebrows that she was glad she had never plucked, the wingspread nose and ripe, melon lips, and her coloring, sand tan like everyone else in the family. She didn't care anymore that her hair wasn't as 'good' as Toby's. She had her mother's chin, long and proud. The neck of the robe opened to the beginning of the swelling of her full breasts. That was as far as the mirror would let her see. But she knew the rest, loved it all. Somebody else could love her too, if she'd let herself…

She turned away from the mirror and back to the bookshelf, looking for something she could use to read herself to sleep. She pulled out a slim paperback volume of poems – Federico Garcia Lorca. Later, when she had washed up and snuggled down under the covers to read, the book fell open of its own accord and a paper marker fell out. The place it had marked was the end of the introduction, written by an editor or translator, but quoting the poet's own words about himself: 'I write poetry because I want people to love me.'

It was the last night Maurie was there that it came up, completely casually, after dinner, while everyone was still at the table. Luckily, there were only the four of them that night, no guests.

'Guess who I saw in town this morning,' Maurie's mother announced to the table at large. 'Francine Albertson.'

Maurie remembered the Albertsons – neighbors who had once been her parents' best friends, but had moved years ago. She remembered the children – Franny, with the stuffed panda bear she carried everywhere, and the ribbon always untied on her top plait, hanging down in front of her face. Jerry, in a too-big police cap, flinging out his arms to block the sidewalk, shouting, 'Red light!' 'What are Franny and Jerry doing now?' she asked.

Before her mother could answer, her father made a noise – somewhere between a harrumph and a sigh – shaking his head. 'It's a shame about that boy. A real shame. He was such a good-looking kid, too.'

'Jerry? What happened to him?' She imagined a car accident, or his face slashed up by a gang of muggers.

But now Pop had apparently said all he wanted to on the subject. 'Just fell in with the wrong crowd, I guess.' That old adult/kid routine – covering up. And then just to their mother, exactly as if Maurie and Toby were a couple of pre-schoolers and simply wouldn't hear him, 'I felt so bad for Al, when he told me. I didn't know what to say. I don't even know why he told me. What a thing to have happen to a man.'

After he left the room, she turned to her mother, to find her suddenly busy clearing the plates from the table, her lips pressed together into a flat, tight line. She disappeared into the kitchen with her hands full, and almost immediately her voice rose in song.

> *Jesus paid it all*
> *All to him I owe*
> *Sin had left a crimson stain ...*

Maurie turned to Toby. 'What was that all about?'

He met the question with that innocent smile of complicity they'd always shared. 'He's gay,' Toby said. 'Jerry Albertson. I used to run into him on the campus sometimes, when I had that summer job at the bookstore.' He glanced out toward the living room, where their father had turned on the TV, then back at her. 'I guess he came out to his old man.'

She was stunned. She could not, for anything, think what would be the totally natural thing to say. Words stammered out. 'Pop thinks it's that bad?'

'Yeah. All he can see is a blot on the old man's character. A failed father somewhere in the background. Fathers are responsible for everything, you know.' He chuckled. Dropped his voice. 'Mom has a much less Freudian outlook: It's a sin. Whatever the question was – Jesus is the answer.'

She ought to be able to laugh along with him, joke about this. She hadn't seen the Albertsons in ten years. None of them should matter to her, at all. There was a tremor in her voice, asking, 'What do *you* think?'

'Me?' He shrugged. 'I think it's the twentieth century. I've been to Greenwich Village.'

She tried to steal a glance at him, and met his eyes. They

were no longer laughing, but steady and thoughtful. She couldn't go on with this conversation, couldn't let him watch her face for another minute. He was too sharp, knew her too intimately. She got up and began to gather the serving dishes, following her mother into the kitchen.

So now she knew what it would be like. Mom would think she was a sinner. Dad would think he was a failure. Only Toby…but she could never tell, not even Toby. She'd have to lie to them for the rest of her life. It felt like lying already, like she'd been lying ever since she got here.

'You put the food away. I'll wash,' she told her mother. And ran the water hard so she wouldn't have to talk just now.

V

Twelve long hours on the bus, to ask herself questions. Framingham, Worcester…not sleeping, watching the shopping malls and parking lots, and then the silent dark fields slip by. Springfield, Albany, Schenectady…unlit farmhouses, lighted cloverleafs, on and off the throughway…Amsterdam, Johnstown, Utica.

Of course, Mom had wanted her to stay. 'I don't understand why you have to leave today, Maureen. It's only *Friday!* We've hardly even had a chance to see you. What do you have to go back so soon for?'

'I just need to be able to spend the weekend at home.' She watched her mother's face draw in, at the word 'home,' and she hurried on. 'I've got to have my lesson plans done by the time school starts Monday. The kids'll be really high, and I want to have my act together.' Another lie.

Oneida. Syracuse. A couple of sleepy-eyed college students – a boy and a girl – gathered together their hats, backpacks, book bags, a stray glove, a guitar. Just the way they collected their belongings, either of them grabbing whatever was closest, made her think that probably they lived together. Stumbling groggily down the aisle, they looked too young to be sexually active, 'living in sin', her mother would say…A new thought pulled her fully awake. It was all right if both of you were kids. But if one was an adult, and the other – seventeen? There were laws, of course.

Did it matter? Being a lesbian was against the law, too.

She stared out through the glass at the sleeping streets. Somewhere along the way it had begun to snow. The windshield wipers slogged back and forth in a dull, blunt rhythm, and the questions licked and nudged at the edges of her mind. Was it taking advantage of Gail? Was it Gail, after all, that drew her? Or had she just needed a Gail, a someone…female…? What if nothing more happened between them? Would Maurie still end up a lesbian? Was she one already? Geneva, Canandaigua, all around the Finger Lakes, the long way home.

The woman next to her had fallen asleep and sagged over to take up three quarters of the seat. Maurie's knees and her back ached and there was a splintery knot in her neck. Rochester, finally…Only another hour now, along the canal.

Twelve hours in all, and no answers – only the long yearning to be home, the absolute certainty that the only place she wanted to be was in that gray city on Lake Erie that Gail would be coming home to, this same morning.

Letting herself into the apartment in the gray dawn light, she piled her bags in the kitchen just inside the door, slung her jacket over a chair. She'd meant to go right to sleep and sleep far into the afternoon, but her head was whizzing, whirring. She would put something mellow on the turntable, then brew a pot of camomile tea, and drink it while she read her mail, winding down.

After two cups, after opening all the Christmas cards, she was still on a zingy high. She felt as if she were still in motion, traveling toward some destination just a little beyond her. On her feet now, she moved from one end of the small space to the other, then back again, and finally to the window.

The sky was white, clearing. The snow was finished. Several inches deep, it clung in a curve to the window frame and hooded the fences and ash cans beyond. The alley was a canyon, filled with a river of snow, that would open to other snowlogged streets, flow past banks of bulgy white cars and bushes – everything soft and anonymous, the city taken by storm.

All of a sudden, she was flinging on her things again, pulling tight at her boot laces, drawing them criss-cross over one another, and then throwing open the suitcase, burrowing haphazardly through the Christmas gifts and toilet articles to find her warmest sweater. As she stepped outside, a gust of wind shoved against her back, and she lurched forward a few awkward staggers, then laughed and ran with it, letting it push her in a clumsy run through the drifts up the alley, and on to the Avenue.

Fifteen minutes later, her heart pounding, Maurie stood in the middle of the unploughed street and faced the stone house on Chapin Parkway. There was no one else on the block, no movement about the house. Huge icicles that sparkled like cut crystal hung from the rainpipes and eaves. In the pearl bright morning light, the many windows glistened like ice. There was no trace of the elegant curving drive that swept around the side, or the steps that led up to the main door, between the two tall columns. There was only snow – deep and unruffled, the yard one with the yard next door, the sidewalk and the street: an open sea of snow.

A moment ago, she had thought this her destination, where she was headed this morning once and for all. But her fingers and feet were tingling; she felt full and vibrantly alive, not yet at the end of this venture. She squinted a moment longer at the house, then took a deep breath. The air was as fresh as cold springwater. Her breath rushed out, and she couldn't stop the smile that took over her face. She turned from the house and pushed on, past it.

At Delaware Avenue, Maurie crossed the deserted street against the light, and slogged in through the wide-standing gate to the cemetery. Alone in the open space, she waded deep into the drifts, leaving her mark – trails and twists and figure eights, crazy spirals and mazes no one would ever understand. She sank knee deep in soft banks and slid on the frozen creek. At the top of the hill, where the wind had blown the road almost bare, she spun in dizzy laughing circles under the bright sky. She filled her lungs with the icy air, and called and shouted aloud, stuck her two fingers in her mouth and spurted out a whistle that frightened all the birds from a snow-laden evergreen. And then she sang – in a loud voice that cracked from the long night of silence – the first song that came to her, dancing in the snow.

With a stick broken from a fallen branch, she began to write, in huge letters through the fresh snow. First she wrote 'I love you.' It didn't matter if it didn't keep, if the wind or the sun erased it, or more snow fell to cover it up. Right now, this day, this hour, it was real, it was true – and wonderful. 'I love you,' she wrote again and again, leaving the message, a loud tell-tale secret, all over Forest Lawn. She drew hearts with arrows through them, crooked stars and crescent moons with sleepy smiling faces, wrote her name and wrote the words again.

It was fully daylight now; the sun had broken through. On a last clear patch of snow, by the fence on the expressway side, there was space for one more message. She drew a circle, and added the two more lines that turned it into a woman's symbol. And then another woman's symbol right beside it, overlapping, intertwined. She had seen that design displayed again and again at the women's center – on posters for upcoming events, in the newsletter, on buttons some of the women wore pinned to their clothing…Now she understood that need to display it, to say it somehow.

Her toes were wet, even through her leather boots, her fingers and face numb. Bits of ice clung to her wet mittens, with the dank smell of damp wool. Heading back down the hill, she smiled at the message that greeted her everywhere. It suddenly struck her who the words were really meant for – how right it was that she should be the one to read them, over and over again.

She had made her own trail, and she followed it, the way she'd come – all the way to the Delaware Avenue gate. At the gate she turned back to gather in one last view of this new place, this play-land of sunshine and snow. But the city this Saturday morning seemed a new place too, shimmering and alight, friendly and full of promise, and still soft-edged and vulnerable under its coverlet of snow. A huge yawn pushed her jaws apart, and then another; a long sigh. She crossed the street and ploughed on toward Elmwood Avenue, toward the alley – coming home.

From *Lover's Choice*, published by The Women's Press.

the wedding dress

MARY FLANAGAN

They meet at a dance. It is the Saturday night after Thanksgiving and the York Beach Casino is filled to capacity. Nora wears a white angora sweater which Frank notices right away, because of its contrast with her dark blue eyes and what he likes to call her apple cheeks, a feature which in 1935 is greatly admired.

They spend the rest of the evening in each other's arms. Couples step aside, making way for them as if the whole floor were theirs by right. During the last dance he dares to hold her a little closer.

Nora's brother Jimmy is driving her home. Frank expresses concern about possible snow, the condition of the roads and the number of whiskies Jimmy has consumed. 'Oh it will be all right,' she says, and he suspects that she is not unhappy about going home with this brother of hers. As they separate, Nora sees that Frank's blue serge suit is covered with angora fluff. He looks as if a dozen Easter bunnies have capered on his chest. Nora feels badly but can't help laughing. Frank laughs too, for he is a good-natured man. He is also, like Nora, a sharp dresser. She tells him he can call on her. They part.

Frank presents his sisters with the fuzzy suit. They manage all his domestic difficulties. Always have.

Lizzie and Sadie exchange looks.

'Jimmy! Jimmy stop it!' Nora, in her bathrobe, leans from the bedroom window, trying to shout and whisper at the same time. 'Please Jimmy.'

In the street below, her brother is attempting, as he does every morning at seven thirty, to start the motorcycle which he bought second-hand from the White Mountains Garage.

'Son of a bitch! God damn!' He kicks it. 'God *damn!*' He kicks it again.

'Please Jimmy!'

'You go to hell, Nora.' His breath and the cycle's steam and billow like an enraged dragon's.

'Jimmy, the Floods…' Neighbors have complained. Harrison Avenue is a Methodist stronghold.

'Fuck the Floods,' he shouts and tries, again without success, to jump-start his ornery machine. 'And fuck you too, Nora, you dumb bitch.'

Nora slams the window shut, her hands trembling. She throws herself on the bed which she shares with her sister Frannie and sobs. The continuing racket of the machine serves as a background to Jimmy's curses.

Frank does some investigating. As a reporter for the *Daily Democrat*, he knows how. He is good at it, he enjoys it. And he is acquainted with nearly everyone in the Tri-City area.

What Frank discovers: Nora Winkle is a Methodist (may present problems), born in Belfast. Emigrated to the US in 1913. Mother cleans houses. Father, estranged, works in a box factory in East Rochester. Nora Winkle is the eldest of ten children. She is secretary to Huntley Bates, boss of the paper mill, a good job for a girl of her background. She is known for her contralto voice and her ladylike behavior. Nora Winkle has also been engaged three times and she has broken each engagement. There was even a medical student from Montreal, but she changed her mind and wouldn't have him. They say he had a nervous breakdown.

Nevertheless, Frank feels encouraged. Frank is an optimist.

Poor Nora: a mother to her brothers and sisters, a husband to her mother.

She stops crying. Oh, she thinks, to be alone. Alone in a room with a few nice things, where it's all new and clean and mine. Where ten people and their friends are not continually fighting and needing you to settle the arguments, losing things and asking you to find them.

But there was that one time, that only terrible time when she *was* alone. One afternoon during her last year in High School she came home to find the house empty. She called for them all, called every name, but heard no reply, no complaining, no music or arguments. And she felt her heart tighten then abruptly stop. Alone. A black helmet was descending over her eyes. Her head was cold and her body hot. Alone. She was sweating – or rather perspiring. She caught hold of the bannister as her knees gave way. 'Mama,' she murmured, 'I'm dying.' Slowly she backed out the front door, clutching her books. 'Mama.' She staggered across the front porch and sat on the hammock, unable to move, her eyes searching the street for one of them. Any one. 'Please,' she whispered, 'come home.' Then Frannie and Ellie turned the corner into Harrison Avenue. Just at that moment her grandmother emerged from the house across the street. She was taking her three pugs for their afternoon constitutional. Immediately Frannie and Ellie crossed the road and made for the trunk of a large elm tree where they huddled together.

'Ha!' cried Grammy Glick. 'I see ye. Ye can't hide from me, ye dirty wee things.'

Nora pressed her head against her books. Oh, to be just alone.

Nora goes to the mirror, takes out her curling tongs and crimps her short blonde hair. Even with red eyes, she is, as they say, a stunner. Yes, high color is the thing. And white, very white skin. She is healthy and exercises with Indian clubs. If only she could get rid of the giveaway Irish freckles. The bleaching cream doesn't really work, despite the promises on the package. Might as well admit it and stop spending precious money on it. Be careful, Nora. You are becoming vain. It is such an easy thing to slide into. The Bible says so.

She has a passion for clothes and spends whatever is left after she hands her paycheck over to her mother on fabric and accessories. She haunts the sales. Her sister Lillian is an expert seamstress and at thirteen was already earning cash by mending silk stockings – so cleverly that her work was almost invisible. Together they 'cook up frocks' from the latest fashion magazines.

Do not be vain, Nora, she tells herself again, studying the back of her head with a hand mirror, be grateful. And she is grateful, because she is an American now, the citizen of a great and good country that has agreed to accept her and her boisterous family and be responsible for them; to offer them jobs in box factories, in linen and paper mills, in bleacheries and shoe factories, to teach them to read and write so that they may buy galoshes and orange pekoe tea and second-hand motorcycles. She offers thanks every night when she says her prayers and every Sunday at church.

At eight precisely Nora leaves for the mill. On the street she passes Millie Flood who smiles, as usual, as though she had not been awakened yet again by foul language. 'The Irish cannot control themselves,' thinks Millie Flood. 'God help them.'

Fresh from his bath, Frank dons the shirt so carefully laundered by his sister Lizzie. Frank is not handsome, but Frank has 'got something'. He checks the auburn curls which he fears are beginning to thin. Never mind, he reckons he'll have them for just about as long as he'll need them.

On the cedar chest is a three pound box of Whitman's Sampler. He has discovered that the only woman he has ever loved, and to whom he will be faithful until he dies at the age of seventy-six, is a chocolate addict. He will attend the Democratic City Committee meeting then drive the twenty miles to Rochester to deliver his gift. Deftly he loops his striped tie and adjusts the knot.

It has been a terrible week. The week before Christmas always is. The dress she and Lil have been working on has had to be completely unstitched. Timmy has brought home three friends for an indefinite stay. She trips every morning over the bodies on the landing. Her mother cannot say no to Timmy. His friends love Mrs Winkle and they love her cooking. She is an even more cheerful slave than their own mothers.

Frannie has been sleepwalking again. Clayton Flood, who once found her wandering by moonlight in his vegetable patch, thinks it has to do with changes in the weather. Whatever it is, something must be done about it. She's becoming dangerous.

At 3 a.m. on Wednesday, Nora woke to find her sister standing over her with an old tennis racket. Nora screamed and Frannie fainted. Timmy complained that he'd been looking for that racket for months.

Normally her somnambulistic behavior was merely strange, even funny. Someone would hear her on the stairs and wake everyone else. Whispering, on tiptoe, they would follow her to the cellar and watch by flashlight as she lifted the wooden cover and looked down into the well.

'Gives me the goddam willies,' Jimmy would say.

'Shhhhhhhhh!'

Then on Saturday there was the incident with Uncle Brendan. At fifty, Brendan Beckett still lived with his mother, the monstrous Grammy Glick. Everyone said she'd had eight husbands, only two of which had been legitimate, and that she'd only married Solomon Glick, the Jewish tailor from Boston, in order to sneak her disorderly family into the Land of Opportunity by the back door. No one knew what had happened to Mr Glick, though Frannie was convinced her grandmother murdered him with a chamber pot and fed him to the pugs. At four feet eleven inches, she was the bane of Harrison Avenue and its environs, and her memory still struck fear into the hearts of men, schoolchildren and cats throughout County Down.

Nora knew something really bad was going to happen. The sign had come just after breakfast. From their sitting room, the Winkles could look straight into the Glick kitchen opposite. Harry, Timmy and little Vinnie saw Grammy Glick descend her permanently snow-covered front steps (the Floods complained they were a health hazard). She cast a malevolent glance at number twenty-seven, but she wasn't quick enough. Anyone who happened to be in the sitting room knew exactly when to hit the floor. Off she went with the pugs, knowing she'd been outsmarted and swearing vengeance.

'Close call.' Harry breathed a sigh of relief as he got to his knees and peeked over the window sill to make sure the coast was clear.

'Oh-oh,' he cried. 'Fire! Fire!'

Nora, Mama and Ellie ran to the sitting room where they could watch Uncle Brendan shoving log after log into the big black stove. 'O God help us!' wailed Mrs Winkle, flapping her apron. 'Not again!'

Four columns of flame from the open burners shot as high as the ceiling. Uncle Brendan liked it warm.

They all ran across the street in pajamas and bathrobes, just in time to save number twenty-eight from conflagration. Mrs Winkle tried to make her half-brother understand how upsetting this sort of behavior was. She said that she would have to tell his mother if he went on this way. This made Uncle Brendan very sad. He said he was truly sorry. He would never do such a terrible thing again. But he had promised before, and his promises only brought more disaster in,their wake.

Sure enough, Sunday morning as Nora was grinding cranberries for the relish, she heard the front door open. She knew with an awful certainty who it was. She called for Jimmy who was in the garage, tinkering with the motorcycle, but Uncle Brendan already stood in the kitchen, wild-eyed and wielding an ax. Jimmy burst in. Too late. Uncle Brendan dashed to the sitting room and proceeded to chop down the Christmas tree before they could lay a hand on him.

'Why?' Mrs Winkle wept into her apron. 'Why?' Hearing her, the younger Winkles began to cry, then Harry and finally Nora. All of them crying together and Uncle Brendan too, not understanding.

'What saps,' Frannie observed.

'I must live somewhere else,' thought Nora.

Jimmy said, as he always did, that Uncle Brendan ought to be locked up. And one day he was. He has been in the Concord Hospital for more than twenty years now. Only Harry, Nora's favorite, still visits him. Of course Uncle Brendan has no idea who Harry is.

For once Frank's instincts are not aligned with his famous brain. He jumps the gun and proposes too soon. She isn't ready for this.

'No,' Nora says. Then more kindly, 'It's been an awful week. Just awful.' And then, 'I can't leave Mama.'

'Ah,' Frank thinks and kisses her and cheerfully departs. Now he understands why the three engagements were broken off.

Nora feels badly. She respects Frank, knows he's kind and smart. But she has told him the truth. She cannot leave her mother. A life of hard work and anxiety has left her looking fifteen years older than she is. Already Mrs Winkle wears old ladies' shoes and thick stockings that bag at the ankle. Her hands are twisted and raw with veins a quarter inch high. (All that yellow washing soap, all that bleach and polish and disinfectant and starch.) It isn't possible to abandon her for something as selfish as one's own home, one's own children, one's own husband, one's own wedding dress. Not when she is Little Nora and her mother is Big Nora, and that is how it's been all her life.

She spies the Whitman's Sampler, lies down on the sofa and devours the entire top layer while listening to Rudy Vallee.

'I'm just a vagabond lover…'

Nora hums along. As she bites into a butter cream center she remembers the words of her best friend Vinette. 'It's getting late, Norrie. You're twenty-six.'

She cannot stop eating the chocolate. Chocolate stills her mind and heart.

The next morning she wakes up covered in hives. Mortified, she refuses to come downstairs for a Christmas dinner laid for twenty. Of course there is no tree. Mrs Winkle could not afford another now. Every year the Winkles spend their last penny on Christmas then go into debt for the next eight months.

Harry brings Nora her turkey and cranberry relish in bed. Nora loves Harry best of her six brothers. He was the easiest to rear and is also the one most like her. She'd held him in her arms all the way across the Atlantic while her parents spent the journey in the lavatory. She cannot leave Harry either.

Frank is a smart person. He has 'got something.' This something is not lost on Mrs Winkle and Frank knows it. It has been many years since Mrs Winkle met a man she could trust, and this too is not lost on Frank. He calls her 'Sweetheart' and gives her presents. He always remembers to bring her *The Boston Herald Traveler* which she calls her 'wee book.'

He takes the three youngest Winkles for rides in his Ford and lets them scream and bicker and jump up and down on the back seat. He buys them candy and takes them to Saturday afternoon matinees to watch Tom Mix and Hopalong Cassidy. He, too, is partial to Westerns.

Nora teases him about being in love with Mama. He answers

that he only misses his own Mama who died when he was fourteen.

'Poor Frank,' Nora says and strokes his cheek.

'But I have the girls.'

Oh yes, the sisters.

Frank drives twenty miles four nights a week to see Nora. Much of his visit is spent in the kitchen with Mrs Winkle. He has added 'Honey' and 'Sweetie Pie' and 'Old Darling' to his repertoire of endearments. Nora he calls Nora.

Politics are his obsession, and he talks to Mrs Winkle about them with great animation and in a way she can understand. She likes this. No one has ever talked to her about serious things, aside from dog bites, broken arms and unpaid bills. She listens. She asks questions as she makes the tea and rolls out the pie crust. She does not mind that Frank Murnane is a Catholic and a Democrat. Once such a thing would have been unthinkable, but this is America, the greatest country in the world. None of those bad old feelings here. And good riddance too.

He says there will be a presidential election soon and will she vote? Oh yes, Clayton and Millie Flood (staunch Republicans) always arrange for her to be driven to the polling booths. The Floods are good friends and neighbors. Fine people. Very kind to her and her family. They even introduced her to the Methodist minister, though of course she never has much time for church. Nora and Harry go. They seem to like it. Nora was even in the Salvation Army, did he know? And Harry will soon be a fully-fledged Mason. The minister likes Nora because she has a beautiful voice. At home Vinette plays the piano while she sings. She sings in the choir too. Gets lots of solos. She'd heard her daughter once in church and cried. Where did it come from she wondered, this beautiful voice? Of course Mr Winkle is musical in a way. Played the bagpipes in a Black Watch band. Kilts and all. My she'd been proud of him. But not like Nora. Bagpipes never made her want to cry.

Frank tells her stories of the great FDR, how he saved the country of America that she loves so much and of which she is so happy to be a citizen. Roosevelt is a hero, he says, omitting the fact that it was the great FDR who repealed Prohibition. The youngest Winkles come and listen too. Then Nora then Harry when he returns from a Masons' meeting. They all move to the big dining room table in order to accommodate Jimmy, who has been sulking in his den over a letter from his estranged wife, and Timmy with his three friends. Their supper has been kept warm for them by Big Nora.

The talk moves from politics to poker. Frank tells funny stories of late night sessions and tricks played on slower witted cronies, forgetting the Methodist line on games of chance. But no one minds. The Winkles begin to tell their own stories, all of which involve disasters. They giggle and guffaw and let the children stay up until one. Harry is pleading 'Shhh, shhh, she'll hear us,' then laughing louder than anyone else. But they are not so hysterical as to neglect to turn off the porch and sitting room lights. They want no visits from vindictive grandmothers. One of Timmy's friends falls off his chair and cuts his lower lip which Little Nora treats with mercurichrome. Big Nora brews more tea and produces a banana cream pie.

The Winkles adore Frank. All but Jimmy, who says he's a phoney. He hates the way Frank always calls him Seamus. Who the hell does that Harp think he is? Nora tells him he's just jealous.

New Year's Eve. There is a dance at the York Beach Casino. Frank takes Nora. Alone this time. No siblings. No little Winkles. She looks like a million dollars, a real lady. He's so proud of her. He will still be proud of her when she shrinks and sags and the color has drained forever from her cheeks – especially then.

'Marry me, Nora,' he says as, the objects of every admiring eye, they sway to the music of Glen Glenn and his orchestra.

'I can't leave Mama,' Nora replies.

105

When they arrive home at four in the morning, Nora makes them cold baked bean sandwiches, her favorite after-dance snack which Frank is slowly learning to love.

By spring they are close enough to exchange confidences and make confessions.

'I've raised nine children,' Nora says. 'Each one as it came along. When she was forty-six and told us she was pregnant with Sonny I said, "Oh Mama, not again!" Wasn't that awful of me? I was angry because she wouldn't stop seeing Papa. We were all angry. Except Frannie. She loves her father best. I still feel guilty about saying that.'

Frank likes her trace of brogue. He asks her about Belfast. He wants to know everything. She tells him her first memory. She was Queen of May, the prettiest little girl on Shankill Road – at least that's what they all said. She wore a white dress and a wreath of flowers and sang a song, she can't remember the words, and held the maypole while everyone danced round her, entwining their colored streamers. It was so pretty. But the festivities were brought to a sudden end by a raid of Catholic boys. They threw stones. Then there was a big fight and the police came. All the children ran away scared and crying. Someone, she never knew who, picked her up under his arm and ran with her, her bare legs and feet dangling, all the way to the Winkles' door where he handed her over to Big Nora.

More confessions. About her clothes. She knows it is a vice. The minister said so in church two Sundays ago, and she is sure he was looking straight at her.

'But I don't spend a lot of money on it,' she hurriedly tells Frank, almost as if she were assuring him that she would make a thrifty wife despite appearances. 'Just the little I have left over when I've given my paycheck to Mama.' He says he realizes that. 'Lil and I go to the sales. We look in the magazines and get ideas. We don't even buy the magazines. We read them in the news shop and memorize the photographs of the models.' She does not say that clothes are the only things that are hers alone.

Her clothes and her voice. Vanity.

She does not tell him that her birth forced a marriage between two unsuited people; that no one was sure of her mother's maiden name; that her father was an Orangeman and had jumped many times over the imaginary bodies of dead Catholics; that when she came to America her mother could not read or write. Nora is ashamed of these things. 'I must tell him,' she thinks. And then, 'I must tell him later.'

'Now you confess,' she says, 'Isn't that what good Catholics are supposed to do?'

He pretends to consider the matter.

'I hate my sisters' cooking.' They laugh.

'Well,' she urges after a moment, 'go ahead. There must be more.'

'They'll be leaving soon and know what? I'll be glad.'

'Leaving? Why then you'll be – '

'All alone.'

Alone. In that big wooden house on the corner with its four bedrooms, its three apple trees, its big back yard with the bridlewreath hedge, its large sunny kitchen...

'Sadie's been transferred to the mill in Manchester and Lizzie's finally getting married.'

'Really?'

'There's one more thing.' He hesitates. 'Don't you want to know it?'

'If you want to tell me.' She presses his hand. She looks so appealing, innocent almost. Frank resists the impulse to kiss her. He's never sure how she'll react.

'I've seen you before.'

She looks at him, nervous suddenly, quizzical.

He saw her at a bean supper in South Berwick. Her color was especially high. Vinette accompanied as she sang numbers from their favorite collection, A Treasure Chest of Songs We Love – 'Ben Bolt' and 'Just Before the Battle Mother', 'The Letter Edged in Black' and 'Whispering Hope'. It was the loveliest thing Frank had ever heard.

'Well my goodness. But you shouldn't flatter me.'

He does not tell her that on that night he resolved to capture her voice.

Summer. Excursions to Rye and Wallis Sands and Old Orchard Beach in Frank's black Ford. The youngest Winkles run wild at the Amusement Park. They are completely unmanageable. Frank buys them candy apples and cotton candy and popcorn. On the way home they are sick. They fight and cry and finally fall asleep, their faces sticky and dirty, their noses running, their soiled socks runched down into the backs of their shoes. Nora tries not to be embarrassed. She begs them to blow their noses. She always carries a small packet of Kleenex.

During the drive she holds Frank's hand. She feels better when she holds his hand. She thinks of a large kitchen, three empty bedrooms, a white dress...

Nora cooks Frank a special Sunday lunch. Mama is to rest (she doesn't), and Frannie is to help.

'Please,' Nora begs her brothers, 'no wells.'

They laugh until they remember that Nora takes wells very seriously. They argue that potatoes taste better with wells. But they promise: just for today. Of course they forget. They heap up their mashed potatoes, make large craters in the centre with the backs of their dessert spoons then fill them to overflowing with gravy. They spend a moment enjoying the effect of their accomplishments then mush the potatoes and gravy into a beige soup. Wells.

Frannie sets the table in a leisurely way, practicing a dance step as she does so. Nora inspects her work. She adjusts the salt and pepper shakers by a quarter inch.

'There.' She smiles at Frannie. 'Isn't that better?'

Frannie smashes a saucer on the floor. 'You wanna see a mess?' she cries. 'I'll show you a mess! Clean it up yourself, Miss Just So!'

*

November, 1936. The presidential election. The Floods arrive promptly at nine in their recently polished car to drive Mrs Winkle to the polling station, then to the house she is cleaning that day. They have done so ever since Mrs Winkle moved to number twenty-seven nineteen years ago. Mrs Winkle sits in the back seat thanking them repeatedly for their kindness. They nod and smile and are pleased with her and with themselves. They are killing the two birds of Civic and Christian duty with one stone. It's not every day a person has a chance to do that.

Mrs Winkle votes. The Floods vote. They wait for her, the motor running, as she chats to the mother of one of Timmy's friends. Mrs Mallon hasn't seen her Michael for two weeks and she's getting a welfare report from Mrs Winkle.

'Well,' says Clayton Flood when Mrs Winkle has climbed into the back seat, 'feel better now that you've helped put Landon in the White House?'

'Oh,' says Mrs Winkle, always cheerful, 'I didn't vote for Landon, Mr Flood.'

'You didn't?'

'I voted for Roosevelt.' She smiles, hands folded in her lap, pleased with her wonderful country.

A silence descends which has no effect whatever on Mrs Winkle.

'Bye bye sir, and all the best.' She waves as she steps from the car.

The Floods do not speak to the Winkles for nearly a year.

'When were you happiest, Nora?'

'In the Salvation Army,' she answers promptly.

Frank laughs, but when he sees the expression in her eyes he stops. He tries to be serious.

The Floods introduced her to Captain Daggett. It was one of many efforts to civilize the Winkles. No one but Nora was interested, but her enthusiasm more than compensated for their disappointment. Captain Daggett was taken with her voice. She'd got to sing lots of solos and play the cymbals. She even loved her uniform.

The others were kind and decent people who never spoke ill of anyone and eschewed the drink. Nora admired them. With them she felt protected. It was a world safe from the likes of Jimmy.

'And when have you been happiest?'

'Right now.'

She understands she might not have given the correct answer.

It's official. After dances, drives and amusement parks; after innumerable evenings in the Winkle kitchen and twenty boxes of Whitman's Sampler and Candy Cupboard; after Vinette has warned 'Don't wait too long, Nora. You're twenty-eight'; after Frannie and Lil vow that if she won't have him they'll make a play for him themselves; after the three children beg and plead and Mrs Winkle cries into her apron; after Harry proclaims Frank a wonderful man (he has got Harry an assistant managership at the Ben Franklin five and dime) and promises to drive Mama over to visit Nora twice a week; after thinking for months about the four-bedroom house – empty of sisters – of her own furniture and china cupboard and most of all the wedding dress – the white dress in which she once again will be Queen of May but with no street fighting this time and satin slippers instead of bare feet, and no stranger carrying her home but her own dear Frank – after all this she says yes at last.

Now Frank's Ford is parked outside 27 Harrison Avenue every evening. And now the moment has come which everyone has been dreading. Grammy Glick cannot be put off any longer. At seven forty-five on a Wednesday morning she storms in, the pugs yapping about her long skirts and lunging at Skippy the Winkles' yellow mongrel, and announces that they will not succeed in 'Sweeping her under the carpet', that they are a bunch of damned ingrates and that she insists on meeting this bloody Papist. She announces that she will not be made to wait another day and bangs her cane on the floor, at which the pugs whine and cringe and roll on their backs and Skippy flees, the screen door banging behind him.

Nora has warned Frank and Frank believes he is prepared. He has faith in his charm.

She is waiting for them. She sits in her kitchen by the big black stove, the pugs at her feet, quiet for once, her skirts spread round her like the Queen of the Gnomes. Uncle Brendan is safely locked in his room, for she wants no ructions but those she creates herself. She wants to look long and hard at this Papist. She wants to see an example of this religion which practices idolatry and makes hamburger meat out of Protestant babies.

'Grammy, this is Francis Martin Murnane.'

Grammy Glick does not answer. She leans forward and peers at him as though giving him the evil eye. Frank lets her look.

'Be nice, Grammy. Say hello. Frank's my fiancé.'

'I know that,' she roars. Nora is silent for the rest of the interview.

'You've tricked Little Nora,' (by which she means Mrs Winkle). 'She was always feeble-minded. They'd all a perished without me. Not a brain among em.' She points to the house across the street. ''Twas I got em all in, you know.'

'You're a very smart old woman, Mrs Glick.'

'And don't you just wish I wunt, Mr Murnane. I've got your measure and you know it. You cast a spell on that poor imbecile Little Nora.'

'You've got me there,' he smiles and winks.

'Shameless,' she sniffs. Then she sniffs again. Oh no, thinks Nora, here it comes. She closes her eyes.

Grammy Glick lifts the hem of her black skirt and folds it carefully back over her lap. Underneath is a grey petticoat which once had been white. This too she raises and folds back over her lap. Then she lifts a yellowed petticoat which might once have been pink and repeats the process. Finally she arrives at the red flannel petticoat, the ragged ruffle of which she lifts to her face. With a noise like Captain Daggett's French horn, she blows her nose into the ruffle, examines her achievement and blows again. Then she unfolds the red petticoat and smooths it over her knees. The might-have-been-pink one follows then the grey and lastly the black skirt. Nora can open her eyes now. Grammy Glick turns to her.

'Ye daft thing,' she says. 'You'd give up your religion, surrender your children to the priests, eh? For this *spiv!*'

'Oh Frank,' Nora speaks at last. 'Let's go.'

'Catholics!' she shouts after them. 'Never trust em. They're not Christian.'

'It's true, Frank, isn't it, I'll have to promise to – '

'Plenty of time.' He pats the hand that rests on his arm. 'Plenty of time.'

'It's true, isn't it?' Nora asks Vinette. 'I can't be a Methodist any more. I can't go to my own church or sing in the choir.'

'Nora,' Vinette looks at her hard. 'It's worth it.'

Lizzie and Sadie are calm. They are concerned but they are calm. They would never express disapproval of their brother Frank. But as he leaves to pick up Nora and take her to her first interview with Father Happny, Sadie remarks quietly, 'You know they say the Scotch-Irish have the worst tempers in the world.'

Frank waves and blows a kiss and genially orders them not to wait up. When he's left they discuss the rumor of insanity in the Winkle family.

Sadie and Lizzie have never seen a Protestant church. They treat Protestants with respect, though it is hard for them not to giggle when Toddy McVeigh makes fun of their Bible reading, the fact that their congregations all sing together, and in English, and that they are too cheap to smarten up their churches with a couple of statues.

Father Happny is a kind man. Still, Nora is nervous of him. She has never spoken to a priest before. She says she understands about the children's baptism and education. They will go to the school next door where for eight years they will be taught by those saintly women, the Sisters of Mercy. She understands that they will make their First Holy Communion and their Confirmation here in St Patrick's. Won't it be a wonderful thing, says Father Happny, when she can receive the sacraments with them?

'Wonderful,' says Nora.

He stresses that she need not take instruction immediately, though of course it would be preferable to be married as a Roman Catholic. She agrees, trying not to show her panic.

Frank, she wants to say when they leave, I'm not ready. But he speaks first. 'See? What did I tell you? Plenty of time, plenty of time.'

Frannie is awakened by Nora's sobbing.

'For Christ's sake,' Frannie moans. She puts her arm around her sister's heaving shoulders. 'Come on, Norrie. It doesn't matter that much. I'd get married in a Men's Room if I could marry Frank Murnane.'

'Oh you're disgusting!' Nora cries even harder.

'Well why not?' Frannie squeals.

'Shut up,' hisses Lil at the door. 'Will you just please shut up. Oh-oh. What's the matter, Norrie? Oh no, is it because – '

'It's *because*,' Frannie sighs.

'Look,' Lil embraces Nora. The other two make room for her on the bed. They can see the silhouettes of moving leaves and branches on the green window shade. 'It's not really so important.'

'Naw,' reasons pragmatic Frannie, 'so you can't do it in the big church. What's so bad? The sacristy's still part of the church. I mean God's there too, I suppose, if that's important to you.'

'I don't want to be married in an old sacristy!'

'Shut up,' yells Timmy and bangs on the wall.

'Oh go stick your head in a bucket,' says Frannie.

They can hear Mama in her heavy black shoes going down the stairs. It is 5.30 a.m.

'It's not just the sacristy.' Nora collects herself. 'It's – the dress!'

'Yeah, that stinks,' Frannie agrees.

'His sisters said an off-white suit would be "appropriate".'

'Well, beige is almost white.'

'Beige! With my high color?'

'Your high horse, more like it.'

'Shut up, Frannie.'

'It's as if I'm not good enough,' Nora goes on, 'to wear a proper wedding dress and be married properly in church. It has to be all hidden and quiet somewhere way out back where no one will see. They're ashamed of me. Even Frank – ashamed.'

With her sisters on either side of her, Nora sleeps at last. The alarm goes off at seven. Bravely she rises, crimps her hair, skips breakfast, leaves for work with Mrs Winkle chasing her down the front steps with a cup of tea.

'At least drink this, Nora darlin. Drink it for Mama.'

'She wants beatin not babyin,' shouts Grammy Glick from her porch as she gathers up the pugs' leashes.

All day Nora thinks about the white dress which will exist forever only as an idea. She thinks how terrible a beige suit will be, even with one of those showy orchids pinned to the lapel. She looks awful in beige. Everyone looks awful in beige.

Huntley Bates admires Nora Winkle. She is hard-working, conscientious, honest. Best secretary he's ever had. He decides to give her a wedding present of $200. It is more money than Nora has ever had at one time.

'Well, Honey, you've earned it,' Frank says. He tells her they'll be lucky together. Look, their luck has already begun. Yes, she says, she is holding their luck in her hand, right this minute.

'Wish my sister Lizzie would get lucky.'

'Why?'

'Marriage postponed again.' Lizzie has been engaged for four years to Eddie MacMahon, the local policeman. A nice man with a sick mother.

'Does that mean…?'

'Fraid so, Norrie. It's won't be for long I promise.'

So the house with the four bedrooms will not be empty and hers after all. She will have to share meals, conversation, a kitchen, with a reticent and unsympathetic woman who will be sure to have fixed ideas about how everything should be done.

'Then I think I'll keep on working for a while,' she says, not showing her disappointment but chastening him all the same.

'Sure, Honey. Plenty of time.'

Plenty of time to turn Papist. Plenty of time to share a kitchen with a stranger. And Sadie, it seems, intends to come home every other weekend. And Mrs MacMahon might live forever. Old women went on and on, especially bad-tempered ones. Look at Grammy Glick. No one knew how old she really was, but she had been sixty-nine for an awfully long time.

The luster, Nora thinks, is draining from this beautiful marriage, this Maypole day of her life. What is she doing anyway? She is marrying a man her mother trusts. Nora suddenly feels bound and gagged. Somehow she must restore this seeping luster. She will not allow them to rob her of her May dance. She will not be a demure little beige convert asking to be accepted despite her shortcomings, asking for verification of her existence, married in a sacristy, married in November.

Nora and Lil visit the news shop where they inspect the latest fashion magazines. This time they buy one. They go to Mrs Pappas' Dress Salon, and Nora tries on several items, the seams of which Lil inspects in the dressing room. They tell Mrs Pappas' assistant the dresses are too large. Expressions of regret all round. Back on the street they head for JC Penney's and the patterns department. Lil finds two which she is sure she can chop and change to suit her sister's odd requirements.

'Remember, this is our secret, Lil.' Not even Harry is aware of what's going on in Lil's room and Mama is far too busy to notice. She's cleaning houses and planning the wedding breakfast.

The next day Nora goes to the bank and withdraws half of

Huntley Bates' wedding present. She doesn't take it all. She leaves them half their luck.

She boards a bus for Portsmouth, where she visits the most exclusive department store in southern New Hampshire. There she buys seven yards of the finest silk chiffon which the salesgirl wraps carefully in tissue paper. Her next stop is Carbury's, where she purchases a pair of satin pumps with not too high a heel (at five foot seven, Nora is considered tall for a woman). At Suzette's millinery shop she finds a saucy hat of indeterminate fur. She buys two of them. Lastly she purchases a pair of silk stockings and some underwear. She is home in time to mash the potatoes, set the table and do a pile of ironing before she falls into bed beside Frannie, who knows something's cooking and is burning to find out what.

Lil and Nora spend their evenings locked in Lil's room, from which the sound of the sewing machine can be heard for hours at a stretch.

'I suppose you think this is bad of me, Lil.'

But Lil is not the person to ask. She cares only for the dress as dress. Its moral implications are not her concern. Nora finds this comforting. How hard it will be to leave her sisters. She cannot imagine life without them and is suddenly afraid. She sits staring, the chiffon beautifully bunched in her lap.

'Get a move on, Norrie,' prompts Lil. Nora threads her needle.

The wedding day. Nora wakes at 5 a.m. She lies in bed, something she never does, as if she were waiting for the sounds of the motorcycle and her brother's curses. She feels as though she were flying apart, pieces of her hurtling off in all directions like iron filings, never again to be drawn together by the magnet of her self. She can just make out the dress, completed the night before, hanging on the back of the closet door.

At five forty-five she makes a pot of tea. She would like to sit in the hammock on the front porch and drink it and eat a cold baked bean sandwich, all alone. But Grammy Glick would be sure to see her and scurry round for a confrontation. She goes to the back steps instead, her coat over her bathrobe. She likes the morning and the bright cold. She sits and drinks her tea and looks at the littered driveway. Timmy and his friends have been drinking beer (not allowed in the house), and the bottles still lie scattered where they left them. The cats have been at the trash can. No one remembered to take Skippy for a walk, and he is straining at his tether, having messed copiously by the garage door. Nora gets a paper bag and begins to tidy up. It is instinct, something she doesn't think about, a habitual reaction.

Jimmy emerges, monkey wrench in hand, eager to attack his motorcycle. He sees Nora at work and starts to cry.

'Norrie,' he sobs, putting his arms round her and burying his face in her neck. 'How can you be getting married? You're just a kid.'

Nora laughs and hugs him. 'I'm two years older than you are.' She will not cry, she will not, because if she starts she will never stop.

'You haven't even lived yet. You've just raised brats and gone to church and sung in that goddam choir.'

'Jimmy!'

'What'll we do without you Norrie? Won't be the same here any more. What the hell will we do?'

Four automobiles are lined up outside 27 Harrison Avenue. Timmy's friends have come through and have begged, borrowed and possibly stolen sufficient transport to carry the entire family, minus Grammy Glick, to Great Falls.

The Winkles come out into the November sunshine. Here and there a few leaves the color of dried blood still cling to the black trees. One of the Winkle boys wears his army uniform. Mama is very proud.

Uncle Brendan has been subdued lately, so they are risking it and he is allowed to come. He is not quite sure which of his nieces is getting married, but he is very happy. He beams, a carnation in the buttonhole of his ancient overcoat and black rubbers over his shoes. His mother, whose face is pressed to the kitchen window, has insisted. She scowls at her ungrateful, disorganized family. She has been asked to the wedding but has refused, to the relief of all concerned. She would rather, she says, endure the fires of hell.

She is cursing them all, Harry is certain. He averts his eyes as he gets into the car. He will be driving Nora and Mama and Frannie, whom Nora has asked to be bridesmaid. She hopes this act of kindness and inclusion will somehow touch her sister and encourage her to reform. It doesn't. But she does like the dressing up. Harry will also give Nora away. Everyone is secretly sad that Papa is not here to do it. They know that he too is sad, but no one says anything about it.

The Winkles climb into the cars, arguing about who will sit where. They all get car sick on long journeys and want to be in the front seat. Even if they leave immediately, they will be half an hour late, but then no one really expects them to be on time.

They are now seated. They all lean forward, craning their necks for a glimpse of Nora, who is coming down the front step. No one speaks. She walks slowly toward the first car, giving the neighbors who are lined up across the street the opportunity for a good long look. She allows herself a quick glance in order to check their expressions. A few mouths, including Millie Flood's, hang open.

Finally Jimmy breaks the silence with a whistle.

'You look like a goddam million, Norrie. But why the color?'

'I like it,' she says.

Mrs Winkle cries all the way to St Patrick's. She is remembering all the times she slapped and spanked and shouted at Little Nora. (None but Sonny were spared her lightning corporal punishment.) Then she would hold them and cry, just as she is doing now. Frannie passes her Kleenex and keeps repeating 'Oh come on, Ma.'

'I'm a damn fool, amn't I,' blubbers Mrs Winkle, who has barely noticed Nora's dress.

Harry holds Nora's hand and does not let go until they reach St Patrick's.

Yes, there they are: Lizzie and Sadie in dark brown coats and identical felt cloches. Lizzie wears short, wool-trimmed boots on which she shifts her weight. They could have waited inside, Nora thinks. But they'd rather freeze and make her feel guilty for being late. Immediately she's sorry for being uncharitable. Why is it, she wonders, looking at the sisters, that in the family lottery of looks, brains and charm, one member should emerge such a clear winner? But Frank, she knows, has goodness as well. When she stands beside him in this outrage of a dress, she will look in his eyes and still see goodness. But she will see something else too, and that will be knowledge, a knowledge of her that has been hidden from him until today. And the knowledge will hurt him a little. And she will sense that and feel satisfied.

Everyone enters the church, the Catholics stopping at the holy water fonts to bless themselves. The youngest Winkles gape at the decor. Frannie gives a little snort and gets a quick kick from Harry. The brother and two sisters wait in the vestibule watching the others walk the long dim side aisle to the sacristy where there is barely enough room for them all and where they begin to get warm from the closeness of other bodies.

Nora refuses a coat. She wants to be exposed for as long as possible in her wedding dress, because she will never wear it again.

She stands at the sacristy door, head up, straight back very straight. There is no music. She sees Frank, dapper but uneasy in a new three-piece suit. He is wearing his father's watch. Beside him is his best man, Toddy McVeigh, whom he has known since childhood and who is a fellow member of the Great Falls chapter of the Knights of Columbus.

Everyone turns, expectant smiles on their faces, hankies at the ready. Then they see it: seven yards of deep purple crepe fall in five tiers over Nora's slender body. The tiers are cut on the bias, so that the bottom tier hangs longer on the right side, ending in a graceful point, while the left exposes Nora's black

119

silk leg as far as her knee. The sleeves are trimmed at the wrist in black fur, the same fur as the hat which adorns her head, tilted at a rakish angle and covering the top of her face with a black net veil. The neckline is low and rounded, exposing her collar bones and the white, white skin of her chest. For the first time in her life she has made up her face. (She has always been what they call a clean-cut kid.)

She is a stunner, a million bucks, the classiest dame in the Tri-City area. She should be going to a nightclub – Twenty-One, the Stork Club, El Morocco – those famous places they have read about but will never visit. She could be going to lunch on the arm of a congressman or modeling for a fashion magazine. She could be going to a funeral – the glamorous widow, the bereaved heiress. The one place she could not be going is to her own wedding.

She takes her best-loved brother's arm. They walk toward the small altar adorned with only two candles and two vases of red roses.

Father Happny's bushy eyebrows shoot up nearly to his white hair. He subdues them with difficulty and tries to smile and look benevolent, which he is.

Lil cannot stop studying her masterpiece.

Frannie thinks this the funniest thing she has ever seen.

Jimmy is embarrassed and can't think why.

Mrs Winkle is crying again.

Toddy McVeigh gives the bride a wink.

Lizzie and Sadie exchange looks.

Nora reaches Frank's side. She searches his eyes and finds there what she expects to find.

Uncle Brendan begins to sing 'The Sash My Father Wore'.

The wedding breakfast is over. Nora steps out of the purple dress and hangs it in the closet that is hers no longer. She removes the black pumps and unrolls the black silk stockings. She takes from a hanger the simple, well-cut, inexpensive dusty-rose going-away suit.

'You're not taking the wow-wee-wow dress?' asks Frannie, who has been smoking a cigarette in the bathroom and Nora knows it. She sniffs but makes no comment.

'Should I?'

'Won't you and Frank be stepping out in DC? Lots of nightclubs there I bet.'

'It's not really what we had in mind.'

'You're a snit, Norrie. Marriage hasn't changed you. I feel sorry for Frank.'

Nora doesn't tell her that their big Washington treat will be a visit to the Senate hearings.

'I'm not ever going to wear it again.'

Frannie calculates that this is not the right moment to ask if she can have it. She'll just borrow it while Nora is away.

'That's stupid to let it rot in a trunk. It was expensive.'

'I'm going to give it to my daughter.'

'For her *wedding*?'

Nora closes the closet door firmly and slips into her coat.

'Don't be silly. To play with when she's little.'

'Play? That beautiful – ?'

'Yes. To dress up in. What's a dress for?'

Nora leaves. Frannie locks the door to the room which will be hers alone until Jimmy brings his wife home to live. She kicks off her shoes, lies back on the bed and smokes another cigarette.

From *The Blue Woman*, published by Bloomsbury.

SOLO

LUCY JANE BLEDSOE

I stood on the rim of a huge, perfectly formed bowl, deep with snow. I'd just skied over a pass that, according to my map, was 9,200 feet high. The peaks surrounding me were banked with snowfields that looked blue in the late afternoon High-Sierra light. Massive clouds, the color of pearls, swarmed around the peaks. And I knew exactly what I was – this being on skis in the marrow of wilderness – a human body and nothing more. That was one thing Elizabeth and I agreed on, even in the last couple years – that the goal is to reach that stripped down state where your cells know everything there is to know, where your feelings go so deep they become one simple force, where sorrow and joy become the same thing.

How I missed Elizabeth.

I cut the metal edges of my skis into the ice-crusted snow for balance and then reached into my pocket for a few yogurt peanuts. We'd always saved the yogurt peanuts to eat at the tops of passes, and nowhere else. Next, I checked to make sure the batteries in my avalanche beacon still had juice. What a joke, carrying a beacon on a solo trip. Who would pick up its high-frequency beeps if an avalanche buried me? I guess it was just habit.

Then I looked down into that steep bowl below me. Its snow pack fed a long drainage that in the spring would fan out into half a dozen streams. My destination was the bottom of that drainage. I planned to camp at High Meadow tonight and then ski out tomorrow morning. I scanned the slope for a safe route down. I figured it was about a five-hundred-foot drop.

'Yahooooo!' Elizabeth's voice hollered in my head. I could see her spirit lean forward with that open-mouthed grin of hers that looked more like a shout than a smile. She shoved her ski poles into the snow and flew off the mountain. Elizabeth would have taken what she called the crow's route, straight down. Her tight telemark turns would have made a long, neat squiggle in the snow all the way to the bottom of the bowl. In the meadow below she would glide to a luxurious stop, then purposely fall in a heap, exhausted from her ecstasy.

'Oh, Elizabeth,' I said, missing her foolhardiness with a pain as sharp as this bitter wind. How I longed to lecture her right then: 'Listen, girl, we've had over a foot of fresh snow in the last week. Got it? The snow pack is *weak*. Add to that the fact that this is a leeward slope on a gusty day.'

By now she would have quit listening. Her face would be turned toward the valley and I'd know she was already flying, dead center in that rapture of hers.

And yet, I would go on with my lecture: 'And look at that cornice!' I'd point to the one about ten yards below me right now.

'What cornice?' she might ask, because it really was a small one and nothing subtle ever figured into Elizabeth's world.

'Elizabeth,' I spoke out loud now. 'This is a prime avalanche slope in prime avalanche conditions.'

I think my voice was an outside mantra for her, the droning noise against which she took flight. My words of caution were her starting blocks. If she were here, this would have been her cue. Off she'd sail. I'd watch her back for a few moments and then realize that being stranded on a ridge top in the High Sierra in March, with a storm pending, was a greater risk than skiing an avalanche-prone slope. I'd be forced to follow.

The wind stormed over the pass, interrupting my thoughts and broadsiding me with so much force that I lost my balance and fell. I lay with my skis and legs tangled in the air above me, let my head fall back onto the snow, and watched the clouds. They'd lost their luster and were becoming swarthy. The feeling of knowledge in my cells disappeared and now I felt the opposite, as if I were all spirit, practically not here at all, like Elizabeth. How fast things changed at this elevation.

They found her car, of course. Who could miss it? Her bumper stickers were as loud as she was. This whole trip I'd been trying to imagine where her body might be. Deep in some crevasse. Buried in an avalanche. Or simply sitting in her camp somewhere, dead of exposure. I couldn't help wanting to believe that she had that shouting smile on her face, wherever she was, although even Elizabeth must have learned the meaning of fear in the moments before death. Or had she?

That they hadn't been able to find Elizabeth didn't surprise me in the least. She had always insisted on camping in the most remote places, hiking or skiing far off-trail, and changing her mind after the trip began so that even if we had told folks where we were going, it didn't matter. Perhaps in a month or two, when the snow melted, they would find her body.

Lying in the snow was a bad idea. I managed to get back on my feet and studied the slope again. The day wasn't getting any younger. My emotional state, as changeable as this mountain weather, cleared and the warmth colonized my cells again. I'd made this solo journey as a tribute to Elizabeth, and now I realized how this very moment, looking down at this perfect avalanche slope in the High Sierra, was the essence of Elizabeth. Here was her soul. She lived for this moment of risk. For the first time since we'd had our final falling out, I began to understand that I'd been as dependent on her for danger as she had been on me for safety.

Elizabeth, I think, knew this all along. She'd even tried to tell me that last trip of ours, but I'd been too angry to listen.

Elizabeth and I had been mountaineering partners, off and on, for almost twenty years. We began backpacking together when we were fifteen. I was the crazy one then, wild and daring, wanting to go farther, deeper, longer, faster, later or earlier. But over the years there was a shift. I grew more cautious and Elizabeth grew more reckless. There were several years in there, when her recklessness had caught up with but not yet overtaken mine, that we were perfect partners. We could choose a campsite and make route decisions almost without talking. We shared the implicit understanding that courting the mountains was our first commitment and working as a team got us closer to those peaks.

I noticed her impatience for the first time on a hiking trip in the Brooks Range of Alaska, just a few months after her mother died. She wanted to take a short-cut, bushwhack some ten miles across a spur where we could join our trail again and save thirty miles.

I pointed to the map. 'Elizabeth, that's a cliff. And there aren't enough landmarks to ensure we'd find the trail. What's the hurry, anyway?'

'Don't use my name,' she snapped.

'What?' I must have looked hurt.

'The way you use my name is patronizing. I can read the map. We can scramble up those rocks.'

'You mean that vertical cliff.'

'Oh, geez,' she said but gave in to me. We had several similar encounters that trip, but I attributed her impatience to the recent death of her mother, nothing more.

Yet over the years I watched this impatience grow into a hunger she couldn't satisfy. She took too many inappropriate lovers – a coke head, a sixteen-year-old, several corporate execs – and wanted each of them body and soul. She embraced new spiritual teachers and practices every year, each time with fast conviction. And yet even as she acquired new lovers and gurus, she remained fiercely loyal to a few of her oldest friends, including her brother Nathan and me. Elizabeth searched for the heart of wilderness in every part of her life.

Back then I thought that if she would just slow down she could discover what it was she so badly needed. Now I think that she hungered only for this moment I faced. That in a strange, almost ghoulish way she got what she wanted – to see how far she could take a risk.

My choice now, to ski this prime avalanche slope or to turn around and ski out the three-day route I'd skied in on, was almost exactly like the one that precipitated Elizabeth's and my first all-out fight. We were circumnavigating Mount Adams in the state of Washington in the late spring. Near the end of the trip, we reached a torrential river gushing out of the foot of a glacier. We spent an entire day, at my insistence and to Elizabeth's disgust, searching for a safe crossing. We never found one.

'Our choice,' Elizabeth finally pointed out, 'is backtracking five days, being home late and not completing the circum-navigation, or jumping the river, being home in two days and completing the circumnavigation.' Her gray eyes looked like nails.

'You missed one option,' I added. 'One of us jumps, lands in the river and is washed downstream. The other goes home to tell her family.'

'Oh, shit.' She looked up at Mount Adams as if appealing for understanding and I felt very small, cut out. I was in her way, had come between her and the mountain. And that, I knew, was the one sacrilege she wouldn't tolerate.

'Look,' she deigned to explain. 'Basically, there are two approaches to life. You can mire yourself in precautions as you endlessly try to outwit fate. Or, you can let her fly. There's risk either way. In the first scenario, you might – probably *will* – miss all that is good in life. In the second scenario, you get what you want, but you might not get it for as long as you want. Your choice.'

I watched the chalky white glacial water as she hammered out her opinion. On either side of the river, a reddish moraine had built up, bereft of life. I longed for a forest then, the thick comfort of living things. I felt very alone with my cautious, fearful self. I also felt angry, used. I felt like that moraine, a pile of debris pushed aside by her forging glacier.

We did jump the stream, adrenaline carrying me across a much broader distance than my body could normally go. But nothing was ever the same between me and Elizabeth.

Another blast of icy wind, stronger still than the last one, blew me off my feet. I slid to within one yard of the cornice, my legs and skis once again a tangle. 'Elizabeth!' I shouted. 'I know you're out there! Quit pushing me, you wild woman.'

Then, surprising myself I added, even louder still, 'I love you!' In spite of everything, Elizabeth was as good as these mountains, this wild, stormy sky. She was part of my wilderness. But that didn't mean I had to be crazy, now that she was dead, and go against all common sense and ski this slope.

I had an idea. I'd have to check the map, but I thought that if I backtracked just to the other side of this pass I could go out the south fork drainage and still only lose a day. I could hitchhike to my car from there. It was a good plan. I'd always told my friends that my coming home late meant nothing more than I'd used good sense and changed my route. I had plenty of food and warm clothing.

I got to my feet, without sliding over the lip of the cornice, and skied back to the top of the ridge. The hard wind died down suddenly and now a gentle breeze brushed my face. I stopped at the top to take one last look at the bowl before retreating down the back, gentle side of the pass.

'Yahooooo!' Once again, I saw her spirit fly over the cornice and down the slope.

I remembered the night of our final fight, a year ago, when we were marooned in our tent. I was lying on my stomach, cooking freeze-dried Szechwan chicken on the stove just outside the tent door, my sleeping bag pulled up to my shoulders. Outside, the snow fell thickly in tiny flakes. We'd been stuck in this camp for twenty-four hours already. Elizabeth had a date the following night and wanted to ski out in the morning regardless of the weather. 'It's only fifteen miles,' she'd said.

'Fifteen miles in a white-out.'

She shrugged, 'We've skied this route before.'

'You'd risk your life for a date?' I challenged.

'Yeah,' she grinned, 'if it's hot enough. And this one is. I mean, I'm not talking about okay sex, this is, oh, how can I even explain to you...' She looked up to the ceiling of our tent, searching, as if the English language just didn't contain the words to make me understand.

'Elizabeth!' I said calmly. 'I know what hot sex is. And it's not worth dying in a blizzard for.'

'Then,' she said, snatching off her wool cap. Her short, honey-colored hair was mashed against her head. 'Then you *don't* know what hot sex is.'

'Oh, fuck you!' I yelled. I was so tired of her constant mocking. 'You're a goddamn lunatic!' I managed to pull on my boots and squeeze out of the tent without knocking over the pot of Szechwan chicken cooking on the stove. I stomped around outside in the blizzard for a few moments, fuming.

When I started shaking violently with cold, I returned. She had a novel propped on one knee and the last of our yogurt peanuts in a plastic bag between her legs. The chicken bubbled away, most of the liquid boiled off. She wolfed down the yogurt peanuts one after another, munching loudly.

'What are you doing?' My voice was dry and accusing. 'Those peanuts are for the pass tomorrow.'

'I'm feeding the lunatic,' she answered softly, faking innocence. 'She's hungry.' A bit of chewed up yogurt peanut spewed out of her mouth as she spoke. She held the bag out to me. 'I think your lunatic may be hungry, too. Want some?'

'Oh, fuck you,' I said again. And we were silent the rest of the evening. I lay awake all night reading short stories and looking forward to being rid of Elizabeth at the end of this journey.

By the next morning the sky had cleared and we skied out, Elizabeth happy to be heading back to the Bay Area in time for her hot date. Me, bitter. It was the last trip we took together. She called me occasionally after that, but neither of us suggested any trips. I went with other friends, she went alone. I dreaded the day when she would see our impasse as yet another unexplored territory she must venture into.

I did find some satisfaction in the fact that she didn't take another partner. Yet, in a way, I was even more jealous that she went solo, that she'd stretched to a place I didn't think I could stretch to.

When her brother called me two months ago to ask if I'd heard from Elizabeth, I knew instantly. He figured maybe an impromptu trip to LA. Or that she was camped out at some new lover's apartment. 'Nathan,' I told him. 'I don't think so.' He waited silently for my explanation and I could tell from his breathing that he knew too. I said, 'She'd mentioned a trip in the Trinity Alps last time I talked to her.'

'Who should I call?' Nathan asked dully. I hung up and went over to his apartment. We called the Forest Service and they located her car within five hours. They gave up looking for her body after a week.

For a long time, all I could think was that I had been right and she had been wrong. She was dead, and still I wished I could continue our dispute, find some way of telling her 'I told you so'. Now, as I turned my back on the bowl, deep with snow, preparing to retreat back down the safe side of the pass, I realized just how great my jealousy had been. She was right. My lunatic was hungry.

Suddenly, I turned around again and faced the steep bowl. A pillow of fog nestled in the trees far below. Somewhere beyond was my car.

I dug my poles into the snow. I pushed slowly at first and then and landed squarely on my skis several feet below. I shot downhill, taking the crow's route, straight down. I wasn't a particularly good downhill skier, I'd never learned telemark turns, so I skied a straight, seemingly vertical line, amazed that

I didn't fall. My feet vibrated as they stroked the long slope. My legs felt like springs, supple and responsive. My head roared. Everything was a white blur. I'd never skied so fast in my life.

Then I heard it. A bellowing that drowned out the rush of wind in my ears. I felt the entire mountain thundering under my feet. In the next split second, I saw powder snow billowing up fifty feet in the air. So this was it, I thought, feeling a strange, dead center calm. No one skied faster than a slab avalanche. And yet, as if I could, I crouched down lower, held my poles close to my body, allowed my legs to be even more elastic, and concentrated on the width between my skis.

Then the avalanche overtook me, careening down the slope to my right, missing me by about ten yards. The roar was deafening and the cloud of snow blinded me, but still I skied.

Elizabeth, I thought, perverse in the coolness of my mind, never raced an avalanche down a slope.

I came crashing into the flats of the meadow below the bowl and plunged into the snow, face first. Sharp pain splintered up my nose, across my jaw. I rolled over on my side and gingerly wiped the snow off my face with a wet mitten, touching my cheekbone and forehead. Nothing seemed to be broken, just mashed. I blinked hard to clear my eyes, and finally saw the wreckage of the avalanche to my right; masses of snow that moments ago were as fluid as water and now as set as concrete. I could have been locked in that pile of snow, my beacon transmitting tiny beeps for some chance stranger to pick up. They would have had about thirty minutes, if I was lucky, to locate and dig me out. I stared and stared at that icy rubble as awed as if it were the remains of an ancient temple.

'Oh, god,' I whispered.

My arms and legs felt paralyzed, but slowly I was able to move each limb, bending and straightening until it regained feeling. I rolled over in the snow and tried to get to my feet, but didn't yet have the strength.

I sensed Elizabeth nearby. 'Did you see me?' I asked, still whispering.

Finally I wept, and as I did I thought I heard her laughing, that hard, wild woman laughter of hers. Until I realized it was my own laughter, in concert with my tears, shaking the very centers of my cells, wringing the sorrow out of my pores.

From *Sweat*, published by Seal Press.

OLD ONES BECOME BIRDS

PATRICIA GRACE

She thought of bedsocks like the ones she'd seen at the Martinborough Fair, knitted in double bluegreen – stocking-stitch in the foot, patterned above, with crocheted drawstrings threaded round the ankles. Same pattern as baby booties, only large. Had thought of buying a pair but it was summer then.

The light near the door was on but the rest of the house was dark and beginning to snore. Woman on the mattress on one side of her was tuning up, and on the other side was an old wheezer. Oldies all having early nights. She settled into the sleeping bag trying not to rustle. Rugby socks would've done the trick.

Anyway she was pleased to have found a space in the main sleeping house, knowing that out in the 'barracks' the young ones would be up talking half the night – preparing workshops or just fooling about. Even now she could hear them coming and going, singing, laughing. But only sounds. Far enough away to be soothing as she lay rubbing blood down into her feet. In the morning some of them would be out doing aerobics with Gus. In the morning there'd be ice.

*

The birds started up, but that was later. Before that, before light, in the deep morning, the tuner next to her began rattling her baggage and murmuring to her companion on the far side. The two put on coats and began making their way, feeling each footstep, chatting loud enough for their own old ears about a torch that one of them had and who it belonged to originally and who that person's father and mother were, and who the grandparents were and where they were originally from. The door opened. No light to come in through it but soon there was torchlight jigging away in the direction of the washroom.

By the time the two returned the coughing had started, the talk, the movement to sit up and wait for light, the to-ing and fro-ing in the dark to the showers, whizzing of atomisers. The women made their way in and got back in under their quilts to wait. The shower was good and hot it seemed.

On the other side of her the old wheezer was pulling on socks, putting a coat over his pyjamas and she expected he was going for a shower too. But no, he was making his way to a space between the window and door, tapping the pou and beginning to chant the morning karakia. Around the house others were joining in, picking up for him when his breath ran out, these first birds.

She knew they wouldn't be let off lightly with the invocations, which seemed timeless and unending and so early, old bird. Restful once she'd accepted that there'd be no more sleep for her that morning. She closed her eyes and let the singsong wash, and when she opened them again dawn had been canted in. She lay and waited for full light.

Hard frost, and a few out with Gus doing aerobics guitar-style. Then a cold shower that she was not keen enough to get right under, but she washed and put on most of the clothing she'd brought with her. Back out in the white she found two mates to walk with before breakfast, comparing nights and the state of showers.

They walked in a white world, along white tracks, through white paddocks, by white fenceposts wired silver. Cobwebs in filigree. Glass trees. Her words were carried on white breath telling of the early-early birds, and back on white breath came the telling about the night in the barracks that had been noisy and cold. One of her companions had managed to sleep through it, one hadn't. Sky of steel with sun burning a white hole in it.

Seating had been arranged in front of the meeting house and the old ones had already found their places. They were animated, chirpy, turning their faces to the sun as they waited for the unveiling of the carved stone which was the first event on the programme for the day. Once the words had been said and the kakahu removed the olds led them all by the carved piece so they could all see and touch it. She watched them ahead of her as they clutched about them their coloured shawls and rugs, fluffing them featherly, beaking the ground with their sticks, eyeing from side to side, feet big and spread in hugboots, ugboots, gumboots and shoes.

At the main meeting of the day the elders had a great deal to say on the subject of oral histories. Stories, if that's what it meant. Life, if that's what it meant. Yeh, yeh, they don't mind telling the stories, long as the stories don't get stolen so all those Pakehas go and make money. And don't want their stories thieved by all those archive people too. It's for our own. That's that. Our own mokopuna. Don't want our own people ripping us off too, it's for the kids.

By afternoon the heads were dropping wingward, the birdlids beginning to droop over bird eyes. Up to everybody else those other things – recommendations, delegations, applications, justifications. Had enough of that but we support the idea, the recording of stories so the children will know. Otherwise, if we didn't support it wouldn't be here with a rumatiki and a flu, middle of winter, telling it.

After a while she realised many of the seats were empty. There'd been a quiet exit of olds. In on the mattresses for an hour or two before mealtime she guessed.

Or gone flying.

She looked up. Yes, there they all were in their bird colours. Become birds.

There, beating up into the sky that deepened as their many coloured wings blocked the sun, while from their throats came the chatter, taptap, call, chant, scratch, wheeze.

It wasn't long before she felt herself rising.

From *The Sky People*, published by The Women's Press.

Love poem

GITHA HARIHARAN

The benches and desks in the empty classroom had Neeta covered on all sides. They formed a close, tight square, like an airless box; or like an orderly phalanx of identical blank-faced strangers advancing on her. She stared them down, willing them to turn into something else.

She willed a change of metaphor: solitude; or the possibilities of an empty room, waiting for someone to come in and light the essential spark.

Neeta recited to herself like a charm:

> *There is one hour alone, long as an artery,*
> *and between the acid and the patience of crumpled time*
> *we voyage through*
> *parting the syllables of fear and tenderness*
> *interminably done away with, done to death.*

She had no idea what this meant. But said over and over again, disjointed from its fellow stanzas, the verse described for her the tangible shapes of two recently-acquired familiars: loneliness, and the inescapable finality of being mid-voyage.

These were also, she had discovered in the last few months, versatile lines; capable of dispelling, or at least blunting, the equally potent terrors of full and empty classrooms; or blurring the stray image of a safely enclosed home, which rose in sharp detail every time she got a letter from her mother.

How did Neeta, a newcomer to the city, a mere girl in a protected and protective women's college, learn the power of image, metaphor? To use it to her advantage, make some private connection between what she read and felt, a link her lecturers spoke of so blandly as part of their performance of duty?

The bell would not ring for another five minutes, but Neeta was already in the classroom. It was her second year at the college, so she knew by now what the other girls said about her – Bookworm. She has no choice – look at her oily hair and her thick spectacles. Her bushy eyebrows and her old salwar kameez, as if she is getting ready for bed in her grandmother's house in the village. Then a more knowledgeable, or more charitable girl would say to the others, Don't you know, she is a scholarship student, a few of our students are not from the city. Do you think everyone has parents like ours?

Neeta moved to the front of the classroom, her back straight, resisting the urge to turn and look, to say, I heard that. In her hometown, her family and the neighbours she had known all her life had told her she was a warm and affectionate girl. Though she had no idea if that was an accurate description, it was acceptable. Now, seeing her difference and her insignificance firsthand, she knew the picture still remained incomplete. The only friends she could have sought out, if they would have her that is, would be either the student nuns, or the clannish, burqa-wearing girls who whispered about their engagements in the college toilets. These girls never lasted long, anyway. Suddenly one or the other would disappear, mid-year, and nobody bothered to find out whether she had got married after all.

*

Love Poem

Neeta was always early for Dr Sharma's lecture. The corridors outside buzzed with gossip, opinions, laughter. It was difficult to believe that the same girls who had such ringing voices could be transformed, once in the classroom, into that impenetrable mass of stubborn, or was it apathetic, silence. Ladies, Dr Sharma would plead, his bespectacled eyes blazing with love of literature, how does this poem move you? What image, what symbol does it bring to your minds? The girls would stare back at him, as if they were locked in a conspiracy to be mute, deaf, enemies to the Finer Things of Life. If they were moved, they giggled; the only response that seemed to come to them with ease.

Neeta was not part of this philistine giggling mob. She preferred to sit in the first row (not a sought after location), her back to the other girls. It was easy enough to block them out of her vision; but she was only just beginning to perceive, dimly, like the prelude to a lesson, that she could also banish them from her mind.

Only in Dr Sharma's class did she find it possible to forget, or even relish and revel in the image of her isolation. In the other classes, she too was often a back-bencher but dutifully taking notes – as a scholarship student she could not afford to lag behind. These classes bored her; the text-books said it all anyway. The lectures were merely for her attendance chart (she had got a certificate for 97 per cent attendance last year), fillers to bridge the time between her long hours at the library and her weekly pilgrimage to Dr Sharma's class on Criticism of Poetry.

Neeta had never been drawn to poetry till she won a scholarship to a rather unpoetic women's college in Bombay. Her father, a small-town schoolteacher proud of his liberal views on the education of girls, agreed to let Neeta go to Bombay. Lying in bed in the room she shared with her two younger brothers, she heard her parents through the thin wall, arguing in whispers about her future.

Why can't she study here, whispered her mother, her anger already close to whining. After all, she is not going to study

138

medicine or engineering, it's not as if this is going to help her earn anything.

What do you know of education? her father retorted. And who's worrying about jobs? You have two sons, don't you?

Neeta recalled her father's look of relief when he inspected the college premises. There was not a single man in sight except the watchman; and he stood, armed with a lathi, outside the college gate. Her father was not allowed to inspect Neeta's room; several girls had already moved in. This seemed to confirm his satisfaction. He left her in the hostel lobby with her suitcases, safe in the custody of rules, wardens, and the constant, suspicion-sharpened company of women.

So Neeta, in a haze of triumph undiminished by her mother's sullen resignation, left her childhood behind her; and embarked alone on her higher education, where the medium of instruction was an entirely foreign language.

The college hostel quickly tarnished her triumph. The girls were friendly, as long as you looked like them and spoke like them. They queued up for hours at the pay phone; they read one Mills and Boon romance a day; and they chatted endlessly about clothes and boys. Watching them, from the fringes of their charmed circle, Neeta felt her tongue curl in her mouth. She spoke less and less. Behind the thick glasses, beneath the two thick pigtails, she dreamt more and more. Of anyplace, mostly fictional because she did not want to think of home, but of anything that would take her away from the daily spectacle of girls plucking their eyebrows and straightening their hair with hot irons.

In her second year, Neeta discovered Dr Sharma. He was something of an anomaly in that holy of holies, a strictly segregated 'ladies' college. A man to begin with, anomaly enough. But a man who read poetry as if it flowed with the blood in his veins and lit up his beady little eyes with their fire! He did not believe in the existence of clichés because he could make any word sound exciting; and alive. Inspiration. Lyrical.

Muse. Metaphor. And of course, love.

He came to the college once a week to deliver his lecture. He spoke eloquently of the need to shed conformity and the fear of being an oddity. To be a poet, even to read poetry, he said, you must learn to be unique; to be an individual. The girls gazed at him blankly, but between classes, they speculated endlessly, with greater imagination than they were given credit for, on his personal life. Neeta heard some of the versions. He is separated from his wife. He left her when she was hugely pregnant. He actually has two wives. One to cook and clean, the other for – for fun. Their giggles were interrupted by a short-haired sophisticate, a girl who painted her nails black. You don't know what you are talking about. He's actually a homo. That's why the nuns let him come here.

Soon Neeta stopped listening. She really did not care whether he had three wives or two husbands. It was his mind, she told herself with feeling, his poetry that she was interested in.

She began his reading list in earnest. She would spend hours at night, long after everyone else was asleep, poring over obscure images she could barely understand. As she read more and more in an alien language, the words, even the strange long ones she had never heard spoken, arranged themselves in legible patterns. They expressed for her some anger, some reservoir of passion that she could not label in her home-grown words.

And suddenly it was all worth it. Even the students she usually found herself stuck with – studious types, most of them nuns who had nothing better to do anyway – were bearable because she carried this small but radiant secret in her heart. She knew what Professor Sharma would have called it: a passion for lofty things, a poetic love for life.

These were his favourite phrases. When he said them, his small, thin body leant hard against the table, his balding head glistened with sweat, and his deep, rich voice trembled just a little.

The day he read out a poem by Neruda was a day Neeta would always remember.

> *Because this once, because just once, because*
> *a syllable or an interval of silence*
> *or the unstifled noise of a wave*
> *leave me face to face with the truth*
> *and there is nothing more to interpret,*
> *nothing more to say; this was everything.*
> *Closed were the forest doors.*
> *The sun goes round opening up the leaves*
> *The moon appears like a white fruit*
> *and man bows to his destiny.*

And Dr Sharma bowed to the class. Before his stupefied audience could react, before they were done with gaping at the damp, bald head bent in humility and awe, he rushed out of the classroom, clasping his collection of Neruda to his chest.

He noticed, at last, her loyalty. After the Neruda class, he would single her out in the midst of a lecture. Nothing much, but his nod when he explained an insight, a smile when he described poetic humour, he would gracefully bestow in her direction. For you alone, a kindred soul, he seemed to say.

Thus honoured, Neeta would feel a dull fire begin its course from her toes up her back to her intent, unsmiling face.

He began lending her books she could not find in the library, where all literary life seemed to end with the passing of TS Eliot. She would listen to him, unblinking, in a silence she hoped at least looked intelligent, as he lectured her after the class, the two of them alone in the room. She read poets she had never heard of before – Yevtushenko, Theodore Roethke and Muriel Rukeyser. Her knowledge of love, a firm, hard seed, grew as she read; sprouted little roots in the moist soil she carefully prepared.

Then like a reward for her months of unstinting devotion, he asked her to a poetry reading a friend of his had arranged. She was to meet him at six in the evening, in the room he rented as paying guest.

Neeta was there twenty minutes early. She was so afraid of

being waylaid by a questioning nun, of being late, that she had given herself at least an hour for the bus ride. But here she was, forty minutes after she had left the college hostel unnoticed, ringing his doorbell.

Dr Sharma opened the door himself. She had expected the landlady, and her confusion made her a little breathless, as if she was late. Come in, come in, he said. You're early, I think we have time for a cup of tea.

The door was an independent entrance to his room, a large but dark and dusty one, books lining all the walls, magazines on the floor, the single bed unmade. He bustled about the corner which served as a make-shift kitchen, and he boiled the water for the tea on a small hot-plate.

Neeta looked around surreptitiously. The corners of the room were covered with fine cobwebs which hung like testimonials to the intellectual life. She picked up an anthology from the shelves and sat down on the only chair in the room.

Half an hour later, the tea cups now empty, Neeta finally relaxed. He did understand her love for poetry, her potential for something different which set her apart from the others.

Then suddenly, in the midst of a particularly interesting lecture on ambiguity in modern poetry, he jumped off the bed he had been sitting on, and pacing the floor in front of her, he asked, his eyes intense: But what do you think of when you read a love poem? How does it move you?

It gives me, Neeta began, but he interrupted impatiently, No, no, what does it do to you? Does it excite you?

And without warning, he pulled his kurta over his head, unbuttoned his trousers and pulled them down his legs. He stood before a speechless Neeta, in his yellowing underwear tied with a cord round his waist. Then he pulled the cord and jumped into bed, arranging his naked body as if he was a poet's muse.

Are you moved now? Does the image of my body excite you? The symbol of my desire?

Neeta sat frozen in her chair. She felt nothing; not fear, not indignation, as she sat there looking at his pale, thin, hairless body, his stick-like legs coyly crossed as if to veil the tumescence between them.

He lay there and recited dispassionately at the ceiling, as if the naked body and the lyrical words were a couple of long standing:

> *Suddenly the wind howls and bangs at my shut window.*
> *The sky is a net crammed with shadowy fish.*
> *Here all the winds let go sooner or later, all of them.*
> *The rain takes off her clothes.*

Then Neeta felt, with horror, the wetness on her cheeks, and she got up and ran to the door, not so much to escape his nakedness, but to hide her own. She shut the door behind her quickly, but he did not come after her.

The next week, Neeta forced herself to go to Dr Sharma's class. He sailed in as usual, and began, without preliminaries, without so much as a glance at her face, the lesson for the day.

Today we have, ladies, a special treat: the perfect love poem. I will write it on the blackboard so that you can read it slowly, with pleasure, letting every word seep into your pores.

His back to the class, he wrote on the blackboard:

> *up into the silence the green*
> *silence with a white earth in it*
>
> *you will (kiss me) go*
>
> *out into the morning the young*
> *morning with a warm world in it*
>
> *(kiss me) you will go*
>
> *on into the sunlight the fine*
> *sunlight with a firm day in it*
>
> *you will go (kiss me)*
>
> *down into your memory and*
> *a memory and memory*
>
> *(i) kiss me (will go)*

Love Poem

The chalk scraped against the blackboard, with a rasping sound like a thirsty kiss. The girls giggled every time the word kiss was written. Neeta bent over her notebook. Her hand holding her pen like a firm caress, she wrote on an almost blank page. March 22nd. In memory of the perfect love poem.

From *The Art of Dying*, published by Penguin Books India.

CHemIStRy

CAROL SHIELDS

If you were to write me a letter out of the blue, typewritten, handwritten, whatever, and remind me that you were once in the same advanced recorder class with me at the YMCA on the south side of Montreal and that you were the girl given to head colds and black knitted tights and whose *Sprightly Music for the Recorder* had shed its binding, then I would, feigning a little diffidence, try to shore up a coarsened image of the winter of 1972. Or was it 1973? Unforgivable to forget, but at a certain distance the memory buckles; those are the words I'd use.

But you will remind me of the stifling pink heat of the room. The cusped radiators under the windows. How Madam Bessant was always there early, dipping her shoulders in a kind of greeting, arranging sheets of music and making those little throat-clearing chirps of hers, getting things organised – for us, everything for us, for no one else.

The light that leaked out of those winter evenings filled the skirted laps of Lonnie Henry and Cecile Landreau, and you, of course, as well as the hollows of your bent elbows and the seam of your upper lip brought down so intently on the little wooden mouthpiece and the bony intimacy of your instep circling in air. You kept time with that circling foot of yours, and also with the measured delay and snap of your chin. We sat in a circle – you will prod me into this remembrance. Our chairs drawn tight together. Those clumsy old-fashioned wooden folding chairs? Dusty slats pinned loosely with metal dowels? A cubist arrangement of stern angles and purposeful curves. Geometry and flesh. Eight of us, counting Madam Bessant.

At seven-thirty sharp we begin, mugs of coffee set to one side. The routines of those weekly lessons are so powerfully set after a few weeks that only the most exigent of emergencies can breach them. We play as one person, your flutey B minor is mine, my slim tonal accomplishment yours. Madam Bessant's blunt womanly elbows rise out sideways like a pair of duck wings and signal for attention. Her fretfulness gives way to authority. *Alors*, she announces, and we begin. Alpine reaches are what we try for. God marching in his ziggurat heaven. Oxygen mists that shiver the scalp. Music so cool and muffled it seems smoothed into place by a thumb. Between pieces we kid around, noodle for clarity, for what Madam Bessant calls roundness of tone, *rondure, rondure*. Music and hunger, accident and intention meet here as truly as they did in the ancient courts of Asia Minor. 'Pas mal,' nods our dear Madam, taking in breath, not wanting to handicap us with praise; this is a world we're making, after all, not just a jumble of noise.

We don't know what to do with all the amorous steam in the room. We're frightened of it, but committed to making more. We start off each lesson with our elementary Mozart bits and pieces from the early weeks, then the more lugubrious Haydn, then Bach, all texture and caution – our small repertoire slowly expanding – and always we end the evening with an intricate new exercise, something tricky to bridge the week, so many flagged, stepped notes crowded together that the page in front of us is black. We hesitate. Falter. Apologise by means of our nervy young laughter. 'It will come,' encourages Madam Bessant with the unlicensed patience of her métier. We read her true meaning: the pledge that in seven days we'll be back here again, reassembled, another Wednesday night arrived at, our unbroken circle. Foul-mouthed Lonnie H with her starved-looking fingers ascends a steep scale, and you respond, solidly, distinctively, your head arcing back and forth, back and forth, a neat two-inch slice. The contraction of your throat forms a lovely knot of deliberation. (I loved you more than the others, but, like a monk, allowed myself no distinctions.) On and on, the timid fingerings repeat and repeat, picking up the tempo or slowing it down, putting a sonorous umbrella over our heads, itself made of rain, a translucent roof, temporary, provisional – we never thought otherwise, we never thought at all. Madam Bessant regards her watch. How quickly the time...

In Montreal, in January, on a Wednesday evening. The linoleum-floored basement room is our salon, our conservatory. This is a space carved out of the nutty wood of foreverness. Windows, door, music stands and chairs, all of them battered, all of them worn slick and giving up a craved-for weight of classicism. The walls exude a secretive decaying scent, of human skin, of footwear, of dirty pink paint flaking from the pipes. Half the overhead lights are burned out, but it would shame us to complain. To notice. Madam Bessant – who tolerates the creaky chairs, the grudging spotted ceiling globes, our sprawling bodies, our patched jeans, our cigarette smoke, our outdoor boots leaking slush all over the floor, our long uncombed hair – insists that the door be kept shut during class, this despite the closeness of the overheated air, choking on its own interior odours of jointed ductwork and mice and dirt.

Her baton is a slim metal rod, like a knitting needle – perhaps it *is* a knitting needle – and with this she energetically beats and stirs and prods. At the start of the lessons there seems such an amplitude of time that we can afford to be careless, to chat away between pieces and make jokes about our blunders, always our own blunders, no one else's; our charity is perfect. The room, which by now seems a compaction of the whole grey, silent

147

frozen city, fills up with the reticulation of musical notes, curved lines, spontaneous response, actions, and drawn breath. You have one of your head colds, and between pieces stop and shake cough drops, musically, out of a little blue tin.

Something else happens. It affects us all, even Mr Mooney with his criminal lips and eyes, even Lonnie H who boils and struts with dangerous female smells. We don't just play the music, we *find* it. What opens before us on our music stands, what we carry in with us on our snow-sodden parkas and fuzzed-up hair, we know for the first time, hearing the notes just as they came, unclothed out of another century when they were nothing but small ink splashes, as tentative and quick on their trim black shelves as the finger Madam Bessant raises to her lips – her signal that we are to begin again, at the beginning, again and again.

She is about forty. Old, in our eyes. Not a beauty, not at all, except when she smiles, which is hardly ever. Her face is a somatic oval with a look of having been handled, moulded; a high oily worried forehead, but unlined. A pair of eye glasses, plastic framed, and an ardour for clear appraisal that tells you she wore those same glasses, or similar ones, through a long comfortless girlhood, through a muzzy, joyless adolescence, forever breathing on their lenses and attempting to polish them beyond their optical powers, rubbing them on the hems of dragging skirts or the tails of unbecoming blouses. She has short, straight hair, almost black, and wears silvery ear clips, always the same pair, little curly snails of blackened silver, and loose cheap sweaters that sit rawly at the neck. Her neck, surprisingly, is a stem of sumptuous flesh, pink with health, as are her wrists and the backs of her busy, rhythmically rotating hands. On one wrist is a man's gold watch that she checks every few minutes, for she must be home by ten o'clock, as she frequently reminds us, to relieve the babysitter, a mere girl of fourteen. There are three children at home, all boys – that much we know. Her husband, *a* husband, is not in the picture. Not mentioned, not ever. We sense domestic peril, or even tragedy, the kind of tragedy that bears down without mercy.

Divorce, you think. (This is after class, across the street, drinking beer at Le Piston.) Or widowed. Too young to be a widow, Lonnie H categorically says. Deserted maybe. Who says that? One of us – Rhonda? Deserted for a younger, more beautiful woman? This seems possible and fulfils an image of drama and pain we are prepared to embrace; we begin to believe it; soon we believe it unconditionally.

We never talk politics after class, not in this privileged love-drugged circle – we've had enough of politics, more than enough. Our talk is first about Madam Bessant, our tender concern for her circumstances, her children, her babysitter just fourteen years old, her absent husband, her fretful attention to the hour, her sense of having always to hurry away, her coat not quite buttoned or her gloves pulled on. We also discuss endlessly, without a touch of darkness, the various ways each of us has found to circumvent our powerlessness. How to get cheap concert tickets, for instance. How to get on the pogey. Ways to ride the Métro free. How to break a lease, how to badger a landlady into repairing the water heater. Where to go for half-priced baked goods. Cecile Landreau is the one who tells us the name of the baked goods outlet. She has a large, clean ice-maiden face and comes from a little town out west, in Alberta, a town with a rollicking comical name. She gets a laugh every time she mentions it, and she mentions it often. A lively and obstinate girl – you remember – and highly adaptive. She moved to Montreal just one year before and already she knows where to get things cheap: discount shoes, winter coats direct from the manufacturer, art supplies marked down. She never pays full price. ('You think I'm nuts?') Her alto recorder, a soft pine-coloured Yamaha, she bought in a pawn shop for ten dollars and keeps it in a pocketed leather case that she made herself in a leathercraft course, also offered at the Y.

The poverty we insinuate is part real and part desire. We see ourselves as accidental survivors crowded to the shores of a cynical economy. By evasion, by mockery, by a mutual nibbling away at substance, we manage to achieve a dry state of asceticism that feeds on itself. We live on air and water or nothing at all; you would think from the misty way we talk we had never heard of parents or cars or real estate or marital entanglements. The jobs we allude to are seasonal and casual, faintly amusing, mildly degrading. So are our living arrangements and our live-in companions. For the sake of each other, out of our own brimming imaginations, we impoverish ourselves, but this is not a burdensome poverty; we exalt in it, and with our empty pockets and eager charity, we're prepared to settle down after our recorder lesson at a corner table in Le Piston and nurse a single beer until midnight.

But Mr Mooney is something else. Hungry for membership in our ranks, he insists loudly on buying everyone a second round, and a third. Robert is his first name, Robert Mooney. He speaks illiterate French and appalling English. Reaching into his back pocket for his wallet, a thick hand gripping thick leather, he's cramped by shadows, blurred of feature, older than the rest of us, older by far, maybe even in his fifties, one of those small, compact, sweet-eyed, supple-voiced men you used to see floating around certain quarters of Montreal, ducking behind tabloids or grabbing short ryes or making endless quick phone calls from public booths.

Here in Le Piston, after our recorder lesson, he drops a handful of coins on the table and some bills, each one a transparent, childish offer of himself. My round, he says, without a shred of logic. He has stubby blackened fingers and alien appetites, also built-up shoes to give himself height, brutal hair oil, gold slashes in his back teeth. We drink his beer down fast, without pleasure, ashamed. He watches us, beaming.

All he wants is a portion of our love, and this we refuse. Our reasons are discreditable. His generosity. His age. His burnished leather coat, the way it fits snugly across his round rump. His hair oil and puttied jowls. Stubble, pores, a short thick neck, history. The way the beer foam nudges up against his dark lip. Any minute he's likely to roister or weep or tell a joke about a Jew and a Chinaman or order a plate of *frites*. The joke, if he tells it, we'll absorb without blinking; the *frites* we'll consume down to the last crystal of salt. Dispassionate acts performed out of our need to absolve him. To absolve ourselves.

Robert Mooney is a spoiler, a pernicious interloper who doesn't even show up until the third Wednesday when we've already done two short Mozart pieces and are starting in on Haydn, but there he is in the doorway, his arms crossed over his boxer's chest. A shuffling awkward silence, then mumbled introductions, and bad grace all around except for Madam Bessant who doesn't even notice. Doesn't even *notice*. Our seven stretches to eight. An extra chair is found, clatteringly unfolded and squashed between yours and Pierre's. (Pierre of the cowboy boots and gold earring, as though you need reminding.) Into this chair Mr Mooney collapses, huffing hard and scrambling with his thick fingers to find his place in the book Madam Bessant kindly lends him until he has an opportunity to buy one of his own.

Layers of incongruity radiate around him: the unsecured history that begs redemption, rough questions stored in silence. How has this man, for instance, this Robert Mooney, acquired a taste for medieval instruments in the first place? And by what manner has he risen to the advanced level? And through what mathematical improbability has he come into contact with Mozart and with the gentle Madam Bessant and the YMCA Winter Enrichment Program and with us, our glare of nonrecognition? When he chomps on his mouthpiece with his moist monkey mouth we think of cigars or worse. With dwindling inattention he caresses his instrument, which is old and beautifully formed. He fingers the openings clumsily, yet is able to march straight through the first exercise with a rhythm so vigorous and unhesitating you'd think he'd been preparing it for months. He has nothing of your delicacy, of course, nor Pierre's even, and he can't begin to sight read the way Rhonda can – remember Rhonda? Of course you remember Rhonda, who could forget her? Mr Mooney rides roughshod over poor Rhonda, scrambles right past her with his loud marching notes blown sharply forward as if he were playing a solo. 'Bon,' Madam Bessant says to him after he bursts through to the end of his second lesson. She addresses him in exactly the same tone she uses for us, employing the same little fruited nodes of attention. 'Clearly you know how to phrase,' she tells him, and her face cracks with a rare smile.

The corners of our mouths tuck in; withholding, despising. But what is intolerable in our eyes is our own intolerance, so shabby and sour beside Madam Bessant's spontaneously bestowed praise. We can't bear it another minute; we surrender in a cloudburst of sentiment. And so, by a feat of inversion, Robert Mooney wins our love and enters our circle, enters it raggedly but forever. His contradictions, his ruptured history, match our own – if the truth were known. Seated at the damp table at Le Piston he opens his wallet yet again and buys rounds of beer, and at the end of the evening, on a slicked white street, with the moon shrunk down to a chip, we embrace him.

We embrace each other, all of us, a rough huddle of wool outerwear and arms, our cold faces brushing together, our swiftly applied poultice of human flesh.

It was Rhonda of all people, timorous Rhonda, who initiated the ceremonial embrace after our first lesson and trip to Le Piston. Right there on the sidewalk, acting out of who knows what wild impulse, she simply threw open her arms and invited us in. We were shy the first time, not used to being so suddenly enfolded, not knowing where it would lead. We were also young and surprised to be let loose in the world so soon, trailing with us our differently coloured branches of experience, terrified at presuming or pushing up too close. If it had been anyone other than Rhonda offering herself, we might have held back, but who could refuse her outspread arms and the particularity of her smooth camel coat? (Do you agree? Tell me yes or no.) The gravest possible pleasure was offered and seized, this hugging, this not-quite kiss.

Already after three weeks it's a rite, our end-of-evening embrace, rather solemn but with a suggestion of benediction, each of us taken in turn by the others and held for an instant, a moonlit choreographed spectacle. At this moment our ardour grows dangerous and threatens to overflow. This extemporaneous kind of street-love paralyses the unsteady. (The youth of today would snort to see it.) One step further and we'd be actors in a shabby old play, too loaded with passion to allow revision. For that reason we keep our embrace short and chaste, but the whole evening, the whole week in fact, bends toward this dark public commerce of arms and bodies and the freezing murmur that accompanies it. Until next week. Next Wednesday. (A passport, a guarantee of safe conduct.) A *la prochaine*.

One night in early March Rhonda appears in class with red eyes. The redness matches the long weepy birthmark that starts beneath her left ear and spills like rubbery fluid down the side of her neck.

You glance up at her and notice, then open your big woven bag for a Kleenex. 'It's the wind,' you say, to spare her. 'There's nothing worse than a March wind.' We're well into Bach by this time and, of all of us, Rhonda handles Bach with the greatest ease. This you remember, how she played with the unsupported facility that comes from years of private lessons, not that she ever mentions this, not a word of it, and not that we inquire. We've learned, even Mr Mooney has learned, to fall back and allow Rhonda to lead us through the more difficult passages. But tonight her energy is frighteningly reduced. She falters and slides and, finally, halfway through the new piece, puts down her recorder, just places it quietly on the floor beneath her chair and runs, hobbling unevenly, out of the room.

Madam Bessant is bewildered – her eyes open wide behind her specs – but she directs us to carry on, and we do, limping along to an undistinguished conclusion. Then Lonnie H goes off in search of Rhonda.

Lonnie H is a riddle, a paradox. Her hair is as densely, dully orange as the plastic shopping bag in which she carries her portfolio of music and the beaded leather flip-flops she wears during class. That walk of hers – she walks with the savage assurance of the young and combative, but on Wednesday night at least she tries to keep her working-class spite in check; you can see her sucking in her breath and biting down on those orange lips.

Later, when we're doing our final exercise, the two of them, Rhonda and Lonnie H, reappear. A consultation has been held in the corridor or in the washroom. Rhonda is smiling fixedly. Lonnie H is looking wise and sad. 'An affair of the heart,' she whispers to us later as we put on our coats and prepare to cross the street to Le Piston. An affair of the heart – the phrase enters my body like an injection of sucrose, its improbable sweetness. It's not what we've come to expect of the riddlesome Lonnie. But she says it knowingly – an affair of the heart – and the words soften her tarty tangle-haired look of anarchy, make her almost serene.

Some time later, weeks later or perhaps that very night, I see Pierre with his waspish charm reach under the table at Le Piston and take Rhonda's hand in his. He strokes her fingers as though he possesses the fire of invention. He has a set of neglected teeth, a stammer, and there is something amiss with his scalp, a large roundness resembling, under the strands of his lank Jesus hair, a wreath of pink plastic. His chin is short and witty, his long elastic body ambiguous. The left ear, from which a gold hoop dangles, is permanently inflamed.

It is Pierre who tells us one evening the truth about Madam Bessant's husband. The story has reached him through a private and intricately convoluted family pipeline: the ex-husband of a cousin of Pierre's sister-in-law (or something of this order) once lived in the same apartment block as Monsieur and Madam Bessant, on the same floor in fact, and remembered that the nights were often disturbed by the noise of crying babies and the sound of Monsieur Bessant, who was a piano teacher, playing Chopin, often the same nocturne again and again, always the same. When the piano playing stopped abruptly one day, the neighbours assumed that someone had complained. There was also a rumour, because he was no longer seen coming or going, that Monsieur Bessant was sick. This rumour was verified one morning, suddenly and terribly, by the news of his death. He had, it seemed, collapsed in a downtown Métro station on a steamy summer day, just toppled off the platform into the path of an approaching train. And one more detail. Pierre swallows as he says it. The head was completely separated from the body.

What are we to do with this story? We sit for some time in silence. It is a story too filled with lesions and hearsay, yet it is also, coming from the artless stammering Pierre, curiously intact. All its elements fit; its sequence is wholly convincing – Monsieur Bessant, swaying dizzily one minute and cut to ribbons the next, people screaming, the body collected and identified, the family informed, heat rising in waves and deforming the future. Everything altered, changed forever.

'Of course it might have been a heart attack,' Pierre says, wanting now to cancel the whole account and go back to the other, simpler story of an unfeeling husband who abandons his wife for a younger woman.

'Or a stroke,' Cecile Landreau suggests. 'A stroke is not all that unusual, even for a quite young man. I could tell you stories.'

Robert Mooney keeps his eyes on the chilly neck of his beer bottle. And he keeps his mouth clapped shut. All the while the rest of us offer theories for Monsieur Bessant's sudden collapse – heat stroke, low blood sugar – Robert keeps a hard silence. 'A helluva shock' is all he says, and then mumbles, 'for her.'

A stranger entering Le Piston and overhearing us might think we were engaged in careless gossip. And, seeing Pierre reach for Rhonda's hand under the table, might suspect carnal pressure. Or infer something flirtatious about Cecile Landreau, toying with her charm bracelet in a way that solicits our protection. And calculating greed (or worse, condescension) in our blithe acceptance of Robert Mooney's rounds of beer. Lonnie H in a knitted muffler, pungent with her own bodily scent, could easily be misunderstood and her cynical, slanging raptures misread. A stranger could never guess at the kind of necessity, innocent of the sensual, the manipulative, that binds us together, that has begun as early as that first lesson when we entered the room and saw Madam Bessant tensely handing out purple mimeographed sheets and offsetting the chaos of our arrival. We were ashamed in those first few minutes, ashamed to have come. We felt compromised, awkward, wanting badly to explain ourselves, why we were there. We came to learn, we might have said had anyone asked, to advance, to go forward, something of that order. Nothing crystallises good impulses so much as the wish to improve one's self. This is one of the things that doesn't change.

After that first night, we relaxed. The tang of the schoolroom played to our affections and so did the heat of our closely drawn chairs, knees almost touching so that the folds of your skirt aligned with my thigh, though from all appearances you failed to notice. The fretfulness with which Madam Bessant regarded her watch put us on our honour, declared meanness and mischief out of bounds, demanded that we make the allotted time count – and so we brought our best selves and nothing else. Our youth, our awkwardness, our musical naiveté yoked good will to virtue, as sacredness attaches itself invisibly to certain rare moments.

I exaggerate, I romanticise – I can hear you say this, your smiling reproach. I have already, you claim, given poor Pierre an earring and a stammer, accorded Lonnie H an orange plastic bag and a sluttish mouth, branded Rhonda with the humiliation of a port-wine birthmark when a small white scar was all she had or perhaps only its psychic equivalent, high up on her cheek, brushed now and then unconsciously with the back of her hand. But there's too much density in the basement room to stop for details.

Especially now with our time so short, five more weeks, four more weeks. Some nights we linger at Le Piston until well after midnight, often missing the last train home, preferring to walk rather than cut our time short. Three more weeks. Our final class is the fourteenth of May and we sense already the numbered particles of loss we will shortly be assigned. When we say good night – the air is milder, spring now – we're reminded of our rapidly narrowed perspective. We hang on tighter to each other, since all we know of consequence tells us that we may not be this lavishly favoured again.

Lately we've been working hard, preparing for our concert. This is what Madam Bessant calls it – a concert. A little programme to end the term. Her suggestion, the first time she utters it – 'We will end the season with a concert' dumbfounds us. An absurdity, an embarrassment. We are being asked to give a recital, to perform. Like trained seals or small children. Called upon to demonstrate our progress. Cecile Landreau's eyebrows go up in protest; her chin puckers the way it does when she launches into one of her picaresque western anecdotes. But no one says a word – how can we? Enigmatic, inconsolable Madam Bessant has offered up the notion of a concert. She has no idea of what we know, that the tragic narrative of her life has been laid bare. She speaks calmly, expectantly; she is innocence itself, never guessing how charged we are by our guilty knowledge, how responsible. The hazards of the grown-up life are settled on her face. We know everything about the Chopin nocturne, repeated and repeated, and about the stumbling collapse on the hot tracks, the severed head and bloodied torso. When she speaks of a concert we can only nod and agree. Of course there must be a concert.

It is decided then. We will do nine short pieces. Nothing too onerous though, the programme must be kept light, entertaining.

And who is to be entertained? Madam Bessant patiently explains: we are to invite our friends, our families, and these *invités* will form an audience for our concert. A *soirée*, she calls it now. Extra chairs have already been requisitioned, also a buffet table, and she herself – she brings her fingers and thumbs together to make a little diamond – she herself will provide refreshments.

This we won't hear of. Lonnie H immediately volunteers a chocolate cake. Robert Mooney says to leave the wine to him, he knows a dealer. You insist on taking responsibility for a cheese and cold-cuts tray. Cecile and Rhonda will bring coffee, paper plates, plastic forks and knives. And Pierre and I, what do we bring? – potato chips, pretzels, nuts? Someone writes all this down, a list. Our final celebratory evening is to be orderly, apt, joyous, memorable.

Everyone knows the fourteenth of May in Montreal is a joke. It can be anything. You can have a blizzard or a heat wave. But that year, our year, it is a warm rainy night. A border of purple collects along the tops of the warehouses across the street from the Y, and pools of oily violet shimmer on the rough pavement, tinted by the early night sky. Only Madam Bessant arrives with an umbrella; only Madam Bessant *owns* an umbrella. Spinning it vigorously, glancing around, setting it in a corner to dry. *Voilà*, she says, addressing it matter-of-factly, speaking also to the ceiling and partially opened windows.

We are all prompt except for Robert Mooney, who arrives a few minutes late with a carton of wine and with his wife on his arm – hooked there, hanging on tight. We see a thick girdled matron with square dentures and a shrub of bronze curls, dense as Brillo pads. Gravely, taking his time, he introduces her to us – 'May I present Mrs Mooney' – preserving the tender secret of her first name, and gently he leads her toward one of the folding chairs, arranging her cardigan around her shoulders as if she were an invalid. She settles in, handbag stowed on the floor, guarded on each side by powerful ankles. She has the hard compact head of a baby lion and a shy smile packed with teeth.

Only Robert Mooney has risked us to indifferent eyes. The rest of us bring no one. Madam Bessant's mouth goes into a worried circle and she casts an eye across the room where a quantity of food is already laid out on a trestle table. A cheerful paper tablecloth, bright red in colour, has been spread. Also a surprise platter of baby shrimp and ham. Wedges of lemon straddle the shrimp. A hedge of parsley presses against the ham. About our absent guests, we're full of excuses, surprisingly similar – friends who cancelled at the last minute, out-of-town emergencies, illness. Madam Bessant shrugs minutely, sighs, and looks at her watch. She is wearing a pink dress with large white dots. When eight o'clock comes she clears her throat and says, 'I suppose we might as well go through our programme anyway. It will be good practice for us, and perhaps Madam Mooney will bear with us.'

Oh, we play beautifully, ingeniously, with a strict sense of ceremony, never more alert to our intersecting phrases and spelled out consonance. Lonnie H plays with her eyes sealed shut, as though dreaming her way through a tranced lifetime, backward and also forward, extending outward, collapsing inward. Your foot does its circling journey, around and around, keeping order. Next to you is Robert Mooney whose face, as he puffs away, has grown rosy and tender, a little shy, embarrassed by his virtue, surprised by it too. Rhonda's forehead creases into that touching squint of hers. (You can be seduced by such intense looks of concentration; it's that rare.) Cecile's wrist darts forward, turning over the sheets, never missing a note, and Pierre's fingers move like water around his tricks of practised tension and artful release.

And Mrs Mooney, our audience of one, listens and nods, nods and listens, and then, after a few minutes, when we're well launched, leans down and pulls some darning from the brocade bag on the floor. A darkish tangle, a lapful of softness. She works away at it throughout our nine pieces. These must be Robert Mooney's socks she's mending, these long dark curls of wool wrapped around her left hand, so intimately stabbed by her darting needle. Her mouth is busy, wetting the thread, biting it off, full of knowledge. Between each of our pieces she looks up, surprised, opens her teeth and says in a good-natured, good-sport voice, 'Perfectly lovely.' At the end, after the conclusion has been signalled with an extra measure of silence, she stows the socks in the bag, pokes the needles resolutely away, smiles widely with her stretched mouth and begins to applaud.

Is there any sound so strange and brave and ungainly as a single person clapping in a room? All of us, even Madam

Bessant, instinctively shrink from the rhythmic unevenness of it, and from the crucial difficulty of knowing when it will stop. If it ever does stop. The brocade bag slides off Mrs Mooney's lap to the floor, but she still goes on applauding. The furious upward growth of her hair shimmers and so do the silver veins on the back of her hands. On and on she claps, powerless, it seems, to stop. We half rise, hover in mid-air, then resume our seats. At last Robert Mooney gets up, crosses the room to his wife and kisses her loudly on the lips. A smackeroo – the word comes to me on little jointed legs, an artefact from another era, out of a comic book. It breaks the spell. Mrs Mooney looks up at her husband, her hard lion's head wrapped in surprise. 'Lovely,' she pronounces. 'Absolutely lovely.'

After that the evening winds down quickly. Rhonda gives a tearful rambling speech, reading from some notes she's got cupped in her hand, and presents Madam Bessant with a pair of earrings shaped, if I remember, like treble clefs. We have each put fifty cents or maybe a dollar toward these earrings, which Madam Bessant immediately puts on, dropping her old silver snails into her coin purse, closing it with a snap, her life beginning a sharp new chapter.

Of course there is too much food. We eat what we can, though hardly anyone touches the shrimp, and then divide between us the quantities of leftovers, a spoiling surfeit that subtly discolours what's left of the evening.

Robert and his wife take their leave. 'Gotta get my beauty sleep,' he says loudly. He shakes our hands, that little muscular fist, and wishes us luck. What does he mean by luck? Luck with what? He says he's worried about getting a parking ticket. He says his wife gets tired, that her back acts up. 'So long, gang,' he says, backing out of the room and tripping slightly on a music stand, his whole dark face screwed up into what looks like an obscene wink of farewell.

Madam Bessant, however, doesn't notice. She turns to us smiling, her odd abbreviated little teeth opening to deliver a surprise. She has arranged for a different babysitter tonight. For once there's no need for her to rush home. She's free to join us for an hour at Le Piston. She smiles shyly; she knows, it seems, about our after-class excursions, though how we can't imagine.

But tonight Le Piston is closed temporarily for renovations. We find the door locked. Brown wrapping paper has been taped across the windows. In fact, when it opens some weeks later it has been transformed into a produce market, and today it's a second-hand bookshop specialising in mysteries.

Someone mentions another bar a few blocks away, but Madam Bessant sighs at the suggestion; the sigh comes spilling out of an inexpressible, segmented exhaustion which none of us understands. She sighs a second time, shifts her shopping bag loaded with leftover food. The treble clefs seem to drag on her ear lobes. Perhaps, she says, she should go straight home after all. Something may have gone wrong. You can never know with children. Emergencies present themselves. She says good night to each of us in turn. There is some confusion, as though she has just this minute realised how many of us there are and what we are called. Then she walks briskly away from us in the direction of the Métro station.

The moment comes when we should exchange addresses and phone numbers or make plans to form a little practice group to meet on a monthly basis perhaps, maybe in the undeclared territory of our own homes, perhaps for the rest of our lives.

But it doesn't happen. The light does us in, the too-soft spring light. There's too much ease in it, it's too much like ordinary daylight. A drift of orange sun reaches us through a break in the buildings and lightly mocks our idea of finding another bar. It forbids absolutely a final embrace, and something nearer shame than embarrassment makes us anxious to end the evening quickly and go off in our separate directions.

Not forever, of course; we never would have believed that. Our lives at that time were a tissue of suspense with surprise around every corner. We would surely meet again, bump into each other in a restaurant or maybe even in another evening class. A thousand spontaneous meetings could be imagined.

It may happen yet. The past has a way of putting its tentacles around the present. You might – you, my darling, with your black tights and cough drops – you might feel an urge to write me a little note, a few words for the sake of nostalgia and nothing more. I picture the envelope waiting in my mailbox, the astonishment after all these years, the wonder that you tracked me down. Your letter would set into motion a chain of events – since the links between us all are finely sprung and continuous – and the very next day I might run into Pierre on St Catherine's. What a shout of joy we'd give out, the two of us, after our initial amazement. That very evening a young woman, or perhaps not so very young, might rush up to me in the lobby of a concert hall: Lonnie H, quieter now, but instantly recognisable, that bush of orange hair untouched by grey. The next day I imagine the telephone ringing: Cecile or Rhonda – why not?

We would burrow our way back quickly to those winter nights, saying it's been too long, it's been too bad, saying how the postures of love don't really change. We could take possession of each other once again, conjure our old undisturbed, unquestioning chemistry. The wonder is that it hasn't already happened. You would think we made a pact never to meet again. You would think we put an end to it, just like that – saying good-bye to each other, and meaning it.

From *Various Miracles*, published by Fourth Estate.

the world with love

ALI SMITH

On a day when it looks like rain and you're wandering between stations in a city you don't know very well, you meet a woman in the street whom you haven't seen for fifteen years, not since you were at school. She has three children with her, one of them is even quite old, nearly the age you were when you were both friends, a girl who looks so like her mother did then that you shake your heads at each other and laugh. You tell each other how well you both look, she asks you about your job, you ask her about her children, she tells you she's just bought a sweatshirt with the name of the city on it for her daughter (they're visiting for the day) but she's refusing to wear it and it cost nearly twenty pounds. Her daughter, thin and determined-looking, glares at you as if daring you to make any comment at all. She reminds you so much of the girl you knew that your head fills with the time she smashed someone's guitar by throwing it out of the art room window, and you remember she had a dog called Rex. You decide not to mention the guitar and ask after the dog instead. He died ten years ago, she tells you.

Then neither of you is quite sure what to say next. You're about to say goodbye when she says to you out of the blue, God Sam, do you remember that time the Ark went mad?

For a moment you don't know what she's talking about and you picture the animals baying and barking, snarling at each other and at the different species round them, at fat Noah and his family trying to keep the noise down. Then it comes, of course it comes, God yes, you say, what a day, eh? and as you're walking along the road, late for your appointment, it all comes, it all comes flooding back.

The French teacher, the Ark everybody called her because her name was Mrs Flood. She liked you, she liked you especially, you were clever. She liked you so much that you hated her class, you hated it when she asked you, and she always did with that tone in her voice that meant, you won't disappoint me, you'll give me the answer, you'll know what it means, you'll know how to say it. The day she called you Sam instead of your full name in front of all your friends, like she was your friend or something, you were mortified, how dare she. How dare she single you out, how dare she make you seem clever in front of everybody, eventually you began to slip a few wrong answers in, and when you did the other girls had no excuse to give you a hard time afterwards.

Mrs Flood always talking about the beauty of French literature with her singsongy highland island voice, scared of the tough mainland boys and the tough mainland girls, scared of your class even though you were the top stream, not much older than you herself really, her hair rolled up round her ears like the princess in *Star Wars*, her eyes like a shy rabbit, her plastic bangles on her wrist jangling into each other as she wrote beautiful French across the board in round letters, *Echo, parlant quant bruit on maine, Dessus rivière ou sus estan, Qui beauté eut trop plus qu'humaine*, pointing to the verbs with the pointer, *j'aurais voulu pleurer* she wrote, *mais je sentais mon coeur plus aride que le désert*, Sam, can you tell me the names for the tenses? she pleaded, and Sally Stewart's friend Donna poked you in the back and jeered in your ear, so it's *Sam* now is it; it's *Sam* now.

Do you remember the time the Ark went mad? The day you came into the classroom and sat down and got your books out as usual and she was standing at the window, staring out over the playing-fields, ignoring the noise level rising behind her as minute after minute passed, ten, fifteen, and each of you realising that it was as if she didn't even know you were there, she wasn't going to turn round, there wasn't going to be any French today. This was the day that one of the boys had brought in a ball of string and the people in the back rows began to tie all the desks at the back together, a network of string woven between the passageways. Somebody coughed out loud, then someone else made a rude noise and you all laughed in relief, but the Ark didn't move, didn't seem to hear. Then Sally Stewart crept out front and stood there like the teacher, you were all giggling, snorting with laughter, and still the Ark didn't turn round and Sally got braver and braver, touching, moving things around on the teacher's table.

She opened the big black dictionary in the middle, letting the cover hit the table with a crash. The Ark didn't look round, she didn't move, not even then, and Sally Stewart was flicking through it and then she was writing on the board the words *le pénis*, then *le testicule*, *les organes génitaux*, she got bolder, and in a teacher voice she said, I'm taking the class today since Mrs Flood isn't here. Who knows the word for to have it off? Who knows the word for french letters?

The boys were roaring, whistling, shouting, the girls were hissing high-pitched laughs, someone, you can't remember who, pulled the poster of the Eiffel Tower off the wall and it got passed round the class. You were laughing and laughing in that scared way and then you noticed that the new girl Laura Watt in front of you three along wasn't laughing, not at all, she was watching, her eyes were going back and fore from Sally at the board to the woman at the window, the Ark, the shoulderblades in her cardigan, her hands resting on the window-sill and her eyes watching a seagull gliding from the roof of the huts to the field. Laura Watt, the new girl, watching it all from behind her dark straight fringe, her chin on her hand, leaning on her elbow watching it. The girl who even though you hardly knew her had heard you say you liked a song and had made you a tape of the whole album, Kate Bush, *The Kick Inside*, and copied out all the songwords off the back of the sleeve for you in her nice hand-writing, even though you hardly knew her, had hardly spoken to her. The paper with the words on it folded inside the tape box smelt strange, different, of what it must be like to be in her house or maybe her room, it was a scent you didn't want to lose so you found you were only letting yourself fold the pages open when you really needed to know what the songwords were.

Then Mrs Flood turned round and everything went quiet. Sally Stewart froze at the table with her hand on the dictionary, it was Sally Stewart who looked scared now, not Mrs Flood, who was laughing in a croaky way at the words on the board and who came across, cuffed Sally quite gently on the back of the head and gave her a push back to her seat.

Mrs Flood rolled the blackboard up and she read again what Sally had written on it. She added some accents to some e's, she put a chalk line through *les lettres françaises* and wrote above, the word *préservatif*. Then she pushed the board right up and wrote in large letters, bangles jangling in the silence, the words Look Upon The World With Love. Then she sat down at the table.

Write that down, she said, write it all down. Heads bent, you wrote it in your jotters, the words look upon the world with love, then you looked around at each other, and you carried on writing down the words on the board, the sex words Sally had found in the dictionary. You were writing until all of a sudden the Ark slammed the dictionary shut and said firmly, now, get out. Go on, she said when nobody moved, go on, off you go, get out, and slowly, unsurely, you all packed your books up and went, the people at the back had to pick their way through the webs of string tied between the desks, and it wasn't until you were out in the corridor that you opened your eyes wide at your friends around you and you all made faces at each other as if to say God! and it wasn't until you were on the turn of the stairs that you let yourself say out loud God! what was all that about? and laughter broke out, and the whole class was clattering madly down the stairs, so noisy that the secretary came out of the headmaster's office to see what was happening and the class was rounded up and made to sit on the floor in the hall until it was time for the next period, and several of your friends were personally interviewed about it by the headmaster though you weren't. Mrs Flood was off school for three months and when she came back you didn't have her any more though you always smiled hello at her in the corridor even though she was obviously a weirdo. And remembering it all like this you can't help but remember what you had really forgotten, dark Laura Watt, and how once you even followed her home from school, keeping at a safe invisible distance on your racer, you watched her come to a house and go up a path and look in her pockets for a key and open the door and shut it behind her, you stood outside her house behind a hedge across the road for half an hour then you cycled home again, your heart in your throat.

Laura Watt, you had found you were thinking about her a lot. You scared yourself with how much you were thinking about her, and with how you were thinking about her. You thought of her with words that gave you an unnameable feeling at the bottom of your spine and deep in your guts. Because you couldn't even say them to yourself, you wrote lists of them in a notebook and you kept the notebook inside the Cluedo box under your bed. In case anyone were to find it you wrote the words FRENCH VOCABULARY on the cover and you filled it with words for the hands, the arms, the shoulders, the neck, the mouth. Words for the lips, the tongue, the fingers, the eyes, the eyes brown, the hair dark, the horse dark (a joke). Words you could only imagine, words like caresses, *les cuisses*. That word was enough to thrill you for three whole days, staring into space over your supper, your mother irritated, asking you what was the matter with you, you saying angrily, there is nothing at all the matter with me, your father and mother exchanging glances and being especially nice to you all that evening.

At night when everybody else was asleep you went through your pocket dictionary page by page from a to z and wrote in your notebook every word that might be relevant. *L'amie, l'amour, l'anarchie, l'anatomie, l'ange, être aux anges, anticiper*. Your French marks went up even higher, the new teacher, a nice Glaswegian girl who looked a bit like Nana Mouskouri, told you on the quiet (she understood these things) that you were the only person in the class who knew how to use the subjunctive. If it were to happen, she wrote on the board. You all copied it down, you watched the heads bent, the head bent three along and in front, you all copied down the words. If I were to say. If you were to see.

In the end you got the highest mark in the class and the only A for the exam in the whole school, you got the fifth year prize and you chose a copy of DH Lawrence's *The Virgin and the Gypsy* because it had naked people on the front and you and your friends thought it would be funny to see the Provost's face when he had to present you with it on prizegiving night. But on the night of the ceremony the Provost was a bit drunk, he mixed up the pages of his speech and he muddled the order of the prizes, when it was your turn to go up on stage with everybody clapping he gave you a book called *Sailing Small Yachts* and afterwards you had to go round like everybody else trying to find the right book and the owner of the book you'd been given.

Laura Watt was playing the violin at the prizegiving, she was top in music and was going to study it at university. One of the music teachers accompanied her on the piano and she played something by Mozart, you couldn't believe the quickness and slyness of her fingers on the strings and the way the music went through you like electricity, she was really good, everybody clapped, you clapped as loud as you could, you wanted to tell her afterwards, that was really great, you went up to her and she showed you the book the Provost had given her, it was *The*

Observer Book of Tropical Fish. I don't have any tropical fish, she said, I chose an Agatha Christie novel. You both laughed, and you said to her, well done anyway, she was smiling, she said, well done yourself, you're awfully good at French, aren't you? You looked away to the side, shy and caught, you wanted to laugh or something, you said, yes, I am, I think.

Remember that, then, as you stop now, laughing into your hands in the rain, leaning against the wall of a grey office building in this beautiful city. Look around you in wonder again at where you are, remember the first night years ago when you went out with your prize book under your arm and her music still burning in your body, and all the walk home you saw the trees and how their branches met their leaves, the grass edging the pavement beneath your feet, the shabby lamp-posts reaching from the ground into the early night sky; you stopped and sat down where you were on the kerb between two parked cars, you knew the wheels, the smell of the oil, the drain full of litter next to you, the pitted surface of the road and the sky spread above you with its drifting cloud, and the words for every single thing you could sense around you in the world flashed through your head in another tongue, their undersides glinting like quicksilver.

From *Free Love*, published by Virago.

the river and
the red spring moon

PATRICIA DUNCKER

We first noticed that something was wrong early in the morning on the way into town. There is a sharp corner by the farm on the hill with a dangerous hidden gateway, out of which come the tractors, usually backing up, plough first, the curved blades gleaming like spikes on a chariot. I had slowed right down to take the road descending towards the river when we saw the police cars, the ambulance, and the armed men with dogs. The invading presence was ranged along the damp banks. I crawled down the hill in first gear, staring.

The still green river, flanked by geometric lines of poplars, gave nothing away. There were no boats on the surface, no fishermen's umbrellas, curving alien shapes among the reeds. People gathered around their rusty cars on the bridge, watching patiently. It was raining, but nobody moved. They stood silent in the cold, still damp, watching. Along the bank, among the yellow wild irises and cow parsley prowled the gendarmes, prodding the grass. Two dogs sniffed purposefully at the edge, their tails raised like flags. The men in white leaned against the ambulance, smoking. There was no noise, no alarm, just the slight movements of the dogs searching the banks. I stopped the car for a moment and we too became part of the grey frieze of waiting figures. No one spoke to us.

We drove on into town, speculating. Was it an accident or a murder?

Later that night we heard that a prisoner had escaped. Had he swum the river and drowned? If so, he was less than one hundred metres away from the bridge. This hypothesis made no sense and was quickly discounted. Had he been hunted by the police and dogs right up to the river? There was a prison at Saintes. But the nearest institution which most closely resembled a prison was the madhouse in Angoulême. I locked up the doors of the barn and the outhouses, which I usually left open at night.

On the following day the rain fell heavily: slabs of heavy, grey spring rain pounding the geraniums. I relit the fire and spent the morning chopping wood. The temperature dropped. The remaining tulips sagged and splayed open, disintegrating in the mud. We cooked a huge stew and turned on the television. There was nothing about the escaped prisoner on the local news.

The rain had eased to a constant drizzle by the next day, but it was still uncomfortably cold in the morning. We drove into town, eager and curious to see what had happened on the bridge. The glassy green surface of the river lay before us, speckled with drops. There were still cars haunting the banks; rusty, ancient 2CVs and a Renault 21, the boot tied up with frayed string. Old men in old coats stood aimlessly in groups all along the banks. I stopped the car and went up to a woman who was waiting. She leant against the side of a decaying truck, her hair shining slightly with raindrops. We looked at each other for a moment or two. She still wore her apron and clogs, as if she had interrupted her work for a while to come down to the bridge.

'What's happened?' I asked.

'Someone has disappeared,' she said.

I nodded and stood beside her in the rain.

'We saw the emergency services,' I said. 'Yesterday.'

'They couldn't find him,' she said, her voice neutral.

I didn't ask who he was. Or if she knew him. Or if he really was an escaped prisoner. I simply stood beside her in the rain, gazing at the river. Then I shook hands quickly, got back into the car and drove on. My hand tingled, as if I had been stung by nettles.

A week later I took the car in for a service. Monsieur Rousseau asked me if there was anything special that needed to be repaired. I didn't think so. I said that there was no hurry and that he could keep the car all day. He drove me back to the farm and as we approached the bridge I told him about what we had seen. Two cars were still there, waiting.

'Ah, you don't know the story?' he said. 'The man who has disappeared used to live on the hill. He was her second husband. Years ago, his brother – it was his brother who was first married to her – drowned in the river. No one knows whether it was an accident or suicide. Same family. Then the widow remarried. She married the younger brother. And now he's gone. They won't find him now. Not until the river rises again. He's probably caught in the reeds at the bottom. The river is very deep, you know, towards the mill. There, it's bottomless. November maybe, they'll find him. The family is from around here. There were fifteen of them, brothers and sisters.'

'How old was he?' I asked.

'Fifty-ish. The dogs found his tracks, leading to the edge of the river.'

'Was it suicide?'

Monsieur Rousseau took his hands off the wheel and waved them about.

'*Alors, là...on ne sait pas.*'

I begin to exchange clichés with the neighbours. '*La pauvre...deux fois dans une vie...mais vous savez, une famille comme ça...c'est quand même bizarre...oui, deux frères...avec des histoires d'accidents, on sait jamais...*' There are no certainties.

It was the time of the red spring moon. The weather remained stormy, rainy, disturbed. We waited for the *saints de glace* to pass. No change was expected before the fourteenth of May. Day after day the chickens pecked in the thick wet grass, retreating to the barn as the rain came down. And every day there were cars still waiting on the bridge. A knot of pilgrims hovering in the dusk, gazing at the green stillness. I nodded to the waiting spectators, but no longer stopped to ask for news. The river yielded nothing.

Then one evening, when the fire was lit and the cats were sleeping peacefully among the cushions, I went out.

It has been raining all day. At eight o'clock the light still hangs in the sky, the water shines on the roadway. I risk going round to the neighbours in boots and hat to ask them if they will feed my cats and chickens while I am in Paris. As I walk back down the road the swifts suddenly surround me in the dusk, looming out of the grey damp, swooping close to the road, rising, curving like fighters against the wall, passing so close that it seems extraordinary I cannot catch them. I stand watching their performance: a troop of acrobats on an invisible trapeze. They rise, arch, dive, rushing against the shutters, balking at the iron gateway, their split tails elegant as evening dress. I become just one more of the obstacles which form the limits of their stage. They pass closer, hurtling straight towards me in a suicidal trajectory, then rising, banking, diving away in the final second before the inevitable collision. Their wing-tips skim the puddles and the curled leaves of the frost-blighted geraniums. The rain begins again and the swifts steady and gather, slowing their extraordinary dance. Suddenly I sense their collective cunning, their intelligence, and I retreat into the gateway, my cheeks burning as if I have been stung. The last one, white front, white mask, hiding the steadiness of his glare, swoops almost against me, pushing me out, forcing me into the courtyard. The sky darkens into twilight. I go inside and shut up all the doors.

The River and the Red Spring Moon

At night, sometimes in the squally gusts of cold rain, sometimes shadowed by the red spring moon, a woman walks along the banks of the river, stepping carefully through the damp grass close to the current. Miles away, I can hear her. But she is not crying. She is singing.

From *Monsieur Shoushana's Lemon Trees*, published by Serpent's Tail and Picador.

CHIPMUNK

JANE ROGERS

There were only two other cars in the car-park. The kiosk where you had to pay for parking was closed up. Gary turned off the engine but stayed in his seat, fingers clasped around the steering-wheel, staring through the windscreen at the low grey sky. Lisa opened her door and got out, steadying herself with one hand on the back of her seat. She made for the trees at the edge of the car-park; he watched in his mirror as she disappeared into them, reappearing a few minutes later.

'Better?'

'Yeah.' She stopped short of getting in, ducking her head into the car to speak to him. 'Fancy a walk?'

'A walk? Here?'

'Well, it's a park isn't it? Must be pretty popular at the right time of year.' She indicated with a tilt of the head, the size of the empty car-park around them.

'All right.'

He got out and started rummaging in the back for their jackets. 'I can only find one of your gloves. D'you want to leave this handbag here – don't you think it'd be safer in the boot?'

'Yeah. Fine. I don't need gloves.'

'It's cold,' he said, leaning in over his seat to wind up her window before locking the door.

'Not very. It's nice to be out in the air.'

He glanced into the car, checking, remembered the camera and unlocked the door again.

'For God's sake.' Lisa moved impatiently towards the board where a map of trails in the park was displayed.

'What d'you say?' he called.

'Nothing. I'll look at the map.'

It was a rustic wooden board with complacent yellow lettering. Rattlesnake Point, the place was called. Three colour-coded trails snaked across the map; they all started from the Information Centre and Café. She crossed the car-park, heading Gary off.

'Found anything interesting?'

'No. The trails begin the other side of the café. Not much to choose between them.'

'We could have a coffee,' he said.

'If it's open.' Lisa plunged on towards the trails.

Probably a mistake to stop here. Another cold grey crappy walk. Rubbing their noses in it. That single-handedly they had managed to choose the worst time of the year to visit Canada. That the much-heralded holiday (honeymoon, they were calling it: didn't eighteen months of living together and not snatching more than a week in Wales, and that with the girls in tow, and the coming of the baby which would probably mean no more abroad for years, entitle this escape to a grander and more romantic name than 'holiday'? Not to mention the visit to Niagara Falls. It *had* to be called honeymoon, so that people would laugh in the right way); that the much-heralded honeymoon was taken *not in the spring*, as they had imagined, but in the bleak and barren late Canadian winter. They had left England swelling into warm green life; parks full of pink blossom and daffodils; pussy willows turned from silver to dusty polleny gold. Spring certain and arrived. They had caught a plane away from that, to Canada. Where filthy snow still lay compacted at the bottom of the Niagara Gorge, despite the rain; where the wind was freezing and the sky leaden and the grass and trees bleached and leeched by the cold to no-colour, not green not grey not beige not brown – nothing, absence of colour, sodden and colourless as a thing washed up on a freezing beach. A month earlier and there would have been thrilling snow and ice. A week or two later, they were assured, and it would be hot sudden spring. But now – first week of April – now was the very worst time.

'Good idea,' said Gary, catching her up. 'To get a breath of air.'

A mistake.

'How're you feeling?' he said. 'Not queasy any more?'

'No. Thanks.'

'We're pretty close to Toronto now. Another hour or two is all, I reckon.'

The silence felt churlish. 'Right.'

'We could see a film tonight. Go to the theatre.'

We could do that at home. 'We could ring up Matty's brother, visit some real Canadians.'

'Matty's brother?'

'Yes. You know she gave me his number – he lives in Toronto.'

'Why d'you want to see Matty's brother?'

'I don't especially. She just said to say hello if we were in Toronto. He could tell us what to visit.'

'We've got a guidebook to tell us what to visit.'

'Yes, but sometimes people who live in a place have a better idea of what's what.'

'You think it's a good idea to lumber ourselves with some guy we've never met?'

'Oh forget it.'

The path, which had been twisting between trees, came out at the edge of a black silent lake, with a boardwalk around its marshy perimeter. Gary drew alongside her.

'I'm not being funny. We can call him if you want. I just can't help thinking what a treat it would seem at home to have the girls somewhere else and no work and a whole clear evening to go out or stay home in, and the last thing you'd want would be to get landed with an unknown Canadian.'

'Yes,' said Lisa. 'You're right. I'm sorry.'

'What d'you mean?'

'You're right. We came to be together. It would be silly to phone the Canadian.'

'But you wanted to. You're not interested in us having time together.'

'Yes I am.'

'Lisa, listen to the evidence. *What shall we do tonight?* I say, and you want to ring up a Canadian.'

'I don't want to spend the fucking night with him.'

'Really?'

'You're being pathetic.'

'OK. If I'm being pathetic. What *did* you want?'

'Can't it be something we do *together*? You and I together – go and meet a new person and find out about their city *together*; is that so awful?'

'I don't want to spend the evening exchanging banalities with a bloody Mountie, if I wanted that I could have stayed at home and watched *Due South*.'

'You are beyond belief ridiculous, and I'm not going to talk about it any more.'

'Look, we've got eight days left – '

'Eight,' Lisa said. 'Jesus. Eight more days of having to choose where to go and what to do and how to be *together*. How can we stand it?'

They walked in silence to the viewing platform at the head of the lake, leaned against the rail and stared across. It was peat-black with dead leaves floating, and bare branches reflected in its mirror-still surface. There were no birds, and nothing moved.

'You could almost imagine a bark canoe – ' Lisa began softly, appeasingly, but he turned and walked quickly away ahead of her. She followed, nerves taut with familiar anger.

The trees they were going through now were birch – young, close-growing birch with beautiful silver-white trunks, and strips of bark hanging loose. She pulled one strip gently and it came away; on the inside it was a warm sun-tanned browny pink. The dead leaves on the ground had not rotted but remained as a thick dry brown carpet, where the wind lifted the occasional leaf and sent it scuttling and rattling over the others. She looked ahead through the pale trunks but he wasn't in sight. Oh wonderful. Now he would get lost in some national park the size of Wales that nobody else would even come into till the summer.

She went at her own speed. Her last suggestion had been that they should dump the car. Take it back to a rental place and get the train, cross some of these vast spaces in company and comfort.

'But the car is our freedom,' he'd argued. 'It's the whole point – it's the only way to see a country like this.' He had not bargained on the Lakes being quite so unprepossessing, this time of year; or on Lisa being sick.

'Did you have early morning sickness with the girls?'

'No. It's not early morning.' It wasn't. It was irregularly throughout the day. 'I think it's the combination of twelve weeks and driving. I used to get horribly car-sick as a kid. I guess pregnancy just makes you more queasy generally.'

'You can take pills for car-sickness.'

'Not while I'm pregnant for God's sake!'

He'd been very apologetic after that. 'We could go on the train. I'm sorry, I didn't realise. We *should* go on the train. It's absolute madness driving round and you feeling sick – what could be worse?'

But then he started thinking; what was the point in toiling

across a landscape that was as brown and dead as this one? Why not cut their losses and visit the cities? Why not visit Toronto and Quebec and get a feel for them? Toronto, the guidebook said, was a wonderful city with the greatest racial mix and range of cuisines in the world. It had a skyline to rival New York.

'You don't want to go to the cities,' she said. 'That wasn't why you wanted to come to Canada.'

'I've changed my mind. I don't care what we do as long as we have a good time. We've slogged round Niagara in the rain; now let's do what other people do on holiday. Pamper ourselves. Swim up and down heated swimming pools, feast in exotic restaurants, shop.'

'You'd hate it.'

'Why d'you assume that?'

There was no point in pressing it any further. She hadn't wanted to be pregnant again: he wanted them to have a baby together. She had let it happen. And now she must endure his return display of selflessness. (Gratitude, she reminded herself. Affection. Concern. Bitch to call it a display.) She had a vision of standing in a shop with him, holding up T-shirts with wolves or moose on them, urging him to help her choose for the girls. His impatient smile and glance out of the window. 'Yeah, they're fine. They're all nice – get those.' Pointing at the two closest. 'What next?'

Half an hour in a shop would be too long for him. But he would be outraged if she wasn't having a good time. Driving and being sick was a picnic, in comparison. Her own discomfort seemed to her to be manageable and contained, to leave him free to enjoy himself – while his would infect the week and kill the whole thing dead.

Something moved in the periphery of her vision and she stopped, tilting her face up to the sky. Something huge and black up there. A sudden near-terror.

'Gary!'

'Ye – es?' His call came from not very far away.

'Look up!' At first she had thought a bat – or even, a cloaked figure. Now she could tell it was a bird. The kind that soars; hawk, eagle, bird of prey. The biggest she had ever seen. Gary came crunching through the leaves towards her.

'Isn't it incredible?'

'What is it?'

'A vulture. There's a notice up here – I've just been reading about them – '

She followed him up across a bumpy rise in the ground to the top of a ridge. The view was unexpected; a deep tree-lined canyon, and woods and fields stretching away on the other side. They were on the highest point for miles around. 'Look.'

She read the board. Turkey vultures arrive back from the south in early spring. Have nested at Rattlesnake Point for years. There was a drawing – a hideous bird with a bald vulture's head and evil beak. She looked up again.

'There's two. Three. One down there.'

Two came gliding down like they were on a ski slope – soaring right past Lisa and Gary's amazed faces; big birds, wings six to eight feet across, she could see the individual feathers shifting and tilting in the fan of the nearer wing, as the bird adjusted its position in the air.

'It's like the flaps on a plane's wing.'

'It is,' Gary agreed. 'Exactly.'

A way down the birds began to rise and turn, with one or two languid wing flaps, and then to climb higher up the sky.

'They look so hideous here,' she pointed to the picture, '– and they're so beautiful.'

'More – two more.' Two more came in from the south, dropped, circling, and made their run down the canyon.

'They're enjoying it,' she said.

'Anthropomorphism. They're looking for nesting sites.'

'Yeah. And enjoying it – as much as we enjoy the onerous biological duty of procreation.' She laughed, glancing at him, and watched his still-piqued face break into a smile.

*

At last they turned away from the canyon. 'It must be spring then,' Lisa said. 'It says they come home at the beginning of spring.'

'Yeah. We know. The birds know. They just forgot to tell the weather.'

'I think we can go back this way.'

They walked in silence, the memory of their argument and the coming oppression of Toronto moving in insidiously to flatten the exaltation of the vultures. All around the ground was carpeted with dead and rattling brown leaves, like old dusty cornflakes.

'What's that?'

'Nothing.'

They walked on and then Lisa stopped again. 'It's *running*. That leaf's *running*. Look.'

One crisp brown leaf was bowling and skittering over the surface of the others, with an impossibly sustained movement, as if the wind was behind it and it alone.

'It's *alive*.'

It stopped, a few yards ahead of them. And they could see that it wasn't a leaf but an animal. A leaf-sized, leaf-coloured animal, with the face and shape of a mouse, and a feathery curl of a tail, like a miniature squirrel. It was brown and black, striped, perfect, with brilliant eyes. It was still for long enough to stare at them, then it skittered off again and vanished.

'How *beautiful*. Is it a chipmunk?'

'Now you see it…'

'I never knew they were so quick.'

They waited a bit longer then walked on slowly, passing other rolling and skittering leaves, none of which stopped long enough for them to be quite sure if it was or wasn't.

'I don't want to go to Toronto.'

'I know.'

'How d'you know? I thought you thought you were doing me a favour,' she said.

'Male intuition.'

She laughed. 'Well?'

'Well what?'

'Where shall we go?'

'What you want is for me to choose, and me to be completely responsible when it's not exactly what you hoped for, although you don't care in advance to say what it is you were hoping for.' His voice was light and when she looked at him he was smiling. Maybe it was all right.

'Got it in one.'

'OK. My shoulders are broad – '

'Oooh.' She put on a joke voice. 'I do like a man who's masterful.'

'All right. Let's get the train *north*. We've got time, we can go by train all the way up to Nova Scotia – through Montreal, Maine, New Brunswick – through the northern forests – all the way to the sea. The Gulf of St Lawrence in the last throes of winter – the islands the Highlanders came to after the clearances – there'll be snow and ice and real wilderness, and we can put on all the clothes we own and say fuck to the weather.'

'Oh *yes*.'

'You can stand another week of my company, doing that?'

'I think so.'

'Well thank you for your vote of confidence, ma'am.' He made a sweeping bow and gave her a slightly strained smile.

'It's OK.' For that moment, it was. She tucked her arm into his. 'It'll be good.'

GIRLS ON ICE

HELEN DUNMORE

Ulli has studied the brackish waters of the Baltic in high-school science. She remember field trips when she had to sample and test sea water before reading up on experiments which reported the leaching of DDT from the shores of our great neighbour into the tissues of Baltic herring. Our great neighbour. That was what they'd called the Soviet Union then. Ironic, derisive. That was the way to survive. There are no national borders as far as pollution is concerned, their teacher had emphasized. They should arm themselves with information. It was their future.

But there were so many campaigns. Campaigns against heart disease. Campaigns to solve the energy crisis. Campaigns against alcoholism. They'd been bored kids in caps with ear-flaps, trawling the water to see how many life forms it supported, looking sideways at each other, grinning and giggling. The environment was less fashionable then. She recalls the very words, held in the glassy tissue of boredom like flies in amber. The relatively shallow, brackish waters of the Baltic freeze easily. Leaving aside, as someone had whispered, the fact that it's fucking freezing anyway.

Girls by the Sea

There's a good title for a painting. Or it could be a chapter heading for a novel perhaps? But not a good title for a poem. Girls by the sea. No, it definitely wouldn't work for a poem. You would begin to think of something sad, something elegiac, something long-gone. Long-gone good times.

Girls on Ice

No better. Trying to be ambiguous. Trying too hard. Can anybody trust a story which starts by shoring itself up with double meanings? Perhaps it's only by not having a title at all that you can hold on to the itch of the moment.

It's very cold. A yellow snow-laden wind is just veering round from north to north-east. Ulli and Edith are walking south-west over the ice, out to sea, and now the wind's blowing directly behind them, butting them along, wrapping their long coats around their thighs and knees so it's hard to walk straight. Edith clutches her fur cap down with both hands. She wears a very soft pair of fur-lined leather gloves which once belonged to her grandmother. The surface of the leather is finely crazed with age, but the gloves are supple and warm. Edith can remember holding her grandmother's hand and stroking the fur cuffs of the gloves. Now her own fingers have replaced her grandmother's.

Ulli's family does not have such things to hand on. Gloves made of the finest leather that could be bought. Made to last. And a bargain, really, if you look at it the right way: once acquired, they last through generations, just like money does.

Ulli is all in brilliant Inca wools: a cap of layered colours, a long scarf which she's crossed over her chest and knotted at her back, and a pair of mittens in ochre and terracotta. Her coat is a heavy secondhand wool greatcoat from a church used-goods store. She has dragged it in at the waist with a wide leather belt, and its skirts flap around her ankles. She likes the contrast between her own narrow waist and the wide swirls of heavy cloth.

Both girls wear laced leather boots with strong crêpe soles

which grip well on the ice. The boots are a neat matt black, and they fit tightly around the ankles. They look rather like Edwardian skating-boots, the kind with holes in the bottom into which you screw the blades. The girls share a detestation for parkas in muddy primaries, for built-up snow-boots and thermal caps with ear-flaps, for mittens with strings which run through the armholes, for padded vests and all-in-one zip-up suits in scarlet or turquoise. In fact they avoid all sensible, practical outdoor clothing of the type listed as suitable for high-school cross-country ski trips. Edith will spend hours washing lace in weak tea until it acquires just the right patina of age. Ulli has spent a fortune on silk thermal underwear so that she need not mummify herself in heavy jumpers all through the winter.

Girls on Ice

Here and there the ice surface is churned by tyres. Away to their right a yellow Saab is nosing its way out, squat as a pig truffling for fish. As far as they can see the Baltic has just stopped still as if a traffic policeman has put his hand up.

'It depends on what you mean by love,' says Edith, skirting a Sitka spruce someone has dragged out here with the idea of lighting a bonfire on the ice. But the fire must have fizzled out, or perhaps someone else put a stop to it. One branch of the spruce is charred, that's all, and the ice is puckered up where the fire has touched it.

Ulli pretends not to hear what Edith has said. She wishes she'd never brought up the subject. They've had this conversation so many times. Is Jussi getting hurt, is Edith responsible for this, is there anything anybody can do about it, ought Edith to pull out of the relationship even if it makes Jussi unhappier than ever in the short term...?

And whatever anybody says it doesn't make the slightest difference to Edith. That's just not the way she thinks. From her point of view, everything's fine. Jussi's having a good time. He must be, or else why would he stay with Edith? After all Jussi's free to do as he pleases, isn't he? Nobody is making him stay.

Certainly not Edith. People should relax more, Edith thinks. Why are they always talking about relationships? Either you are having a good time with somebody; or you aren't. If you aren't, talking about it doesn't help. And besides, Jussi is so moody these days. No fun to be with at all.

And Ulli can't help feeling that there's a great deal in what Edith says, even though it does make some of her friends so indignant that they stop discussing relationships with Edith and start shouting instead. There's certainly something lacking in Edith, they say to one another afterwards.

Edith is a fashion student. She's set up her loom in the house where she lives with four other students and she weaves marvellously rough bright cloth out of which she cuts jackets and coats. One boutique is taking her clothes already; though their mark-up is scandalous, Edith says. In a year or two, when she's built up her stock, Edith's going to open a shop of her own, in partnership with two other final-year students. There's no doubt that Edith's going to make it. This winter she's trying out a technique she calls scrap-weaving, and the room where she sleeps is covered with pieces of experimental cloth. She's making up small, close-fitting jackets, like skating jackets. There's a woman in England who breeds a particular type of long-haired sheep, and Edith's got some wool samples from her; Jacobs, the sheep are called. Edith is making drawings of brief, smooth, long-haired skirts.

Girls in Short Skirts

They could walk on the ice in their short skirts, with thick tights and legwarmers and boots. Why not? They'd lose that nipped-in Russian look, that lovely balance of torso and leg, but they'd gain something nice. The sense of striding out.

Men Looking at their Legs

Yes, there'd be that of course. Does Ulli mind? Does Edith mind? Their legs are bold in dark green thick-ribbed tights and diamond-patterned Inca leg-warmers. Their legs are not anybody's easy meat. They have no desire to wear glossy nylon and to strip off their frozen skin along with their tights.

It's nearly too cold to think. They go on squeaking over the ice, not wanting to turn back and walk into the wind. When they look back, the wind slashes at their eyelids until they brim with tears. A curd of snot freezes from Ulli's nostrils to her lips. The shore is so far away. How far they've come, much further than they meant. The town is just a little clutch of houses, humped round by low hills. Ulli feels as if she's swimming miles out. She'd like to lie back and scull the water with her hands. She'd like to float on her back as close as possible to the surface of the water and to the warm sun. She must block out of her mind the dark depths of the water heaving underneath her. When she looks back to shore she feels a shiver of fear, emptiness and weakness, as if her blood is pouring out of her.

Girls on Ice

The only ones out here now. The yellow Saab has crawled back to its heated garage, and the kids who were practising ice hockey and shrieking across the bay to one another have all gone back home to drink hot chocolate and make up their team lists. Because soon it's going to be dark. Already the horizon is folding in all around them. Already the reed banks have gone, and the spruce plantation behind the reeds. Blink, and the dusk thickens. Two soft round lights come on where the town is, and then there are more and more, coming on in warm rooms, as distant and inaccessible as the lights of a liner passing close inshore with a long moo from its foghorn. Blink, and you'll miss the way home.

'We'd better go back,' says Edith.

They turn, and the wind bites into them, glazing each particle of exposed flesh with frozen tears. Ulli's greatcoat flaps open and a knife of wind slides up the inside of her thighs. She trips, and barges into Edith. They just can't walk fast enough. The wind is shoving them offshore, like a flat hand saying BACK, BACK! But they are glad of its noise as it whines and buffets past their ears. They know for sure that they are too far out. The sound of the wind will hide from them what they are afraid to hear: the slow creak and unzipping of the ice. No good telling them now that the ice is solid from here to Ahvennanmaa. Out here you have to believe in ghosts and in ice spirits and broad-backed monsters breaking the surface with their snouts.

The girls link arms. This way it's easier to walk against the wind. They have to keep their heads down.

'Don't keep staring at your boots,' shouts Ulli, 'it'll send you to sleep!'

God, that is the last thing she needs. A sleeping Edith, keeled over on the ice, confident that everything's going to be all right.

It depends on what you mean by love.

A cuff of wind throws the girls sideways. Now there are particles of ice in it. The air's blurring. And surely it isn't quite so cold? The temperature's going up quickly, towards freezing-point.

'I think it's going to snow,' says Edith.

'You don't need to shout about it!' says Ulli. She doesn't want to give the weather any more ideas than it seems to have already. Now she remembers someone telling her that there's a current around here. It curves past the headland and then sweeps in close to shore. You want to watch that you don't get caught. But she didn't take much notice at the time. Who was it told her? It must have been some time last summer. They must have been going swimming, or perhaps Birgit had planned to take the boat out? They hadn't taken any notice. Birgit knew the coast like the back of her hand.

Now Ulli looks up and sees the snow coming from the north-east. The snow rushes towards them like the great filtering mouth of a whale. A ribbed curtain, swaying as it gains on them. The town lights have gone, but Ulli still knows where they were. She clings on to knowing where they were as the snow closes in on Edith and Ulli and wipes out the colours of cap and greatcoat, scarf and bold bottle-green tights until it's all one whirlpool of white. Ulli thinks of the current, a long smooth muscle flexing itself under them. Edith's cap has been torn off by the wind, and her wild brown hair flares upward, crusted with snow, snaking and streaming above her head like the locks of a Medusa. Edith's mouth is wide and her teeth are bared and white. Surely, thinks Ulli, she can't be laughing?

Girls on Ice

If you take a photograph of Edith and Ulli now, they would be dots. Black and white, merging to grey. Look closely and you won't see their images at all, just two darker splodges on a pale background, like a graze on the paper. They'll look as accidental and as unconvincing as those photographs taken to prove the appearance of ghosts.

Enlarged, Edith and Ulli would be cell-like clumps of dots, like embryos held together in the loose grip of one particular moment before the wind changed, before the snow covered them or stopped falling, before they reached or failed to reach the shore.

From *Love of Fat Men*, published by Penguin.

CONTRIBUTORS' NOTES

Margaret Atwood was born in Ottawa in 1939, and grew up in northern Quebec and Ontario, and in Toronto. She has lived in many other cities, including Boston, Vancouver, Edmonton, Montreal, Berlin, Edinburgh and London, and has travelled extensively. She has published over twenty books, including novels, poetry and literary criticism. She lives in Toronto with novelist Graeme Gibson and their daughter Jess.

Toni Cade Bambara was born and brought up in Harlem, New York. She is the bestselling author of *Deep Sightings* and *Rescue Missions: Fiction, Essays and Conversations* (The Women's Press, 1997), edited and introduced by Toni Morrison; two short story collections, *Gorilla My Love* (The Women's Press, 1984) and *The Sea Birds Are Still Alive* (The Women's Press, 1984); and a novel, *The Salt Eaters* (The Women's Press, 1982). Toni Cade Bambara died on 9 December 1995.

Becky Birtha has published two collections of short stories: *For Nights Like This One: Stories of Loving Women* and *Lovers' Choice*

(The Women's Press, 1988). Her stories and poetry have appeared in a number of literary and feminist journals. She currently lives in Philadelphia, where she is working on a novel.

Lucy Jane Bledsoe is the author of *Sweat* (1995), a collection of short stories and a novella, and *Working Parts* (1997), a novel. Her stories have appeared in numerous collections and she has edited several anthologies, including *Goddesses We Ain't: Tenderloin Women Writers* (1992), funded by a San Francisco Women's Foundation Grant, *Let the Spirit Flow*, with Pam Nicholls (1995) and *Heatwave* (1995). She has received a National Endowment for the Humanities Youth grant and the PEN Syndicated Fiction Award. She works as a writer and teaches creative writing workshops for adult literacy programs in the Bay Area.

Angela Carter was born in 1940. She read English at Bristol University, and from 1976 to 1978 was fellow in Creative Writing at Sheffield University. She lived in Japan, the United States and Australia. Her first novel, *Shadow Dance*, was published in 1965, followed by *The Magic Toyshop* (1967, John Llewellyn Rhys Prize), *Several Perceptions* (1968, Somerset Maugham Prize), *Heroes and Villains* (1969), *Love* (1971), *The Passion of New Eve* (1977), *Nights at the Circus* (1984, James Tait Black Memorial Prize) and *Wise Children* (1991). Four collections of her short stories have been published: *Fireworks* (1974), *The Bloody Chamber* (1979, Cheltenham Festival of Literature Award), *Black Venus* (1985) and *American Ghosts and Old World Wonders* (1993); they have been collected together as *Burning Your Boats* (1995). She was the author of *The Sadeian Woman: An Exercise in Cultural History* (1979), and two collections of journalism, *Nothing Sacred* (1982) and *Expletives Deleted* (1992). She died in February 1992.

Patricia Duncker was born in Jamaica. She was sent to England in the mid-1960s and educated at Bedales School. After a spell working in Germany she went up to Newnham College, Cambridge, where she read English and then on to St Hugh's College, Oxford, where she completed her doctorate on English and German Romanticism. She has spent a good part of her life travelling, and has lived and worked in Germany and France, where she still spends part of the year. She now works in the Department of English at the University of Wales, Aberystwyth, where she teaches writing, literary theory and nineteenth century literature. Her critical work includes *Sisters and Strangers: An Introduction to Contemporary Feminist Fiction* (1992). She is the editor of *In and Out of Time: lesbian feminist fiction* (1990) and co-editor, with Vicky Wilson, of *Cancer through the eyes of ten women* (1996) to which she is also a contributor. Her first novel, *Hallucinating Foucault* (1996) won the Dillon's First Fiction Award and the McKitterick Prize. It has been translated into Dutch, French and German. Her first collection of short stories *Monsieur Shoushana's Lemon Trees* was published in 1997.

Helen Dunmore is a novelist, short-story writer and poet. Her novels are *Zennor in Darkness*, awarded the McKitterick Prize in 1994, *Burning Bright*, *A Spell of Winter*, winner of the 1996 Orange Prize for Fiction, *Talking to the Dead* and *Her Blue Eyed Boy*. Her short stories have been collected in *Love of Fat Men*. Her poetry collections include *The Sea Skater*, winner of the Poetry Society's Alice Hunt Bartlett Award, *The Raw Garden*, a Poetry Book Society Choice, and *Secrets*, winner of the 1995 Signal Poetry Award. A selection of her poems can be found in *Penguin Modern Poets 12*. Helen Dunmore was born in Yorkshire and now lives in Bristol with her husband and children.

Mary Flanagan is the author of two novels, *Trust* and *Rose Reason*, and two volumes of short stories, *Bad Girls* and *The Blue Woman*. She lives in London.

Patricia Grace was born in Wellington, New Zealand, in 1937. She is of Ngati Raukawa, Ngati Toa and Te Ati Awa descent, and is affiliated to Ngati Porou by marriage. She has published four collections of short stories: *Waiariki*, which was the first published collection by a Maori woman, came out in 1975 and was followed by *The Dream Sleepers*, *Electric City* and *The Sky People* (The Women's Press, 1995). She has written children's books, of which *The Kuia and the Spider* won the 1982 New Zealand Children's Picture Book of the year; and novels, including *Potiki* (The Women's Press, 1987), winner of the fiction section of New Zealand Book Awards in 1987, and the LiBeraturpreis in Germany in 1994; *Mutuwhenua: The Moon Sleeps* (Livewire Books, The Women's Press, 1988); *Cousins* (The Women's Press, 1993) and *Baby No-eyes* (The Women's Press, 1999). Patricia Grace has taught in primary and secondary schools and was the Writing Fellow at Victoria University in Wellington in 1985. She is married with seven children.

Githa Hariharan was educated in Bombay, Manila and the United States where she also worked in public television. Since 1979, she has worked in Bombay, Madras and New Delhi, first as an editor in a publishing house, then as a freelancer. *The Thousand Faces of Night* (The Women's Press, 1996) won the Commonwealth Writers Prize for the best first novel. Githa Hariharan has also published *The Art of Dying*, a collection of her stories; another novel, *The Ghosts of Vasu Master*, and edited *A Southern Harvest*, an anthology of short stories. Her stories have appeared in magazines and journals internationally, and 'The Remains of the Feast' was included in the anthology, *In Other Words: New Writing by Indian Women* (The Women's Press, 1993). Her new novel *When Dreams Travel* will be published by Picador in 1999.

A.L. Kennedy was born in Dundee in 1965. Her first collection of stories, *Night Geometry and the Garscadden Trains*, won the Saltire Award for best First Book and the *Mail on Sunday*/John Llewellyn Rhys Prize. This was followed by two novels, *Looking for the Possible Dance*, which won a Somerset Maugham Award, and *So I Am Glad*, which won the Encore Award and was joint-winner of the Saltire Scottish Book of the Year Award; and two collections of stories, *Now That You're Back* and *Original Bliss*. In 1993 she was chosen as one of the twenty. Best of Young British Novelists. She wrote the script of the BFI/Channel Four film, *Stella Does Tricks*, and is working on a number of film and drama projects. She lives in Glasgow.

Michèle Roberts was born in 1949 of a French mother and English father. *A Piece of the Night*, published in 1978, was her début novel, and also the first work of original fiction to be published by The Women's Press. It established Michèle Roberts as a major literary writer, and was followed by *The Visitation* (The Women's Press, 1983). Michèle Roberts is now an established and acclaimed writer of poetry and prose, including her sixth novel, *Daughters of the House*, which was shortlisted for the 1992 Booker Prize and won the WH Smith Literary Award 1993. Her eighth novel, *Impossible Saints*, was published in 1997 and her work of essays *Food Sex and God: On Inspiration and Writing* in 1998.

Jane Rogers has written five novels, *Separate Tracks*, *Her Living Image* (winner of a Somerset Maugham award), *The Ice is Singing*, *Mr Wroe's Virgins* and *Promised Lands*. She has also written original drama for television, and adapted *Mr Wroe's Virgins* as a BBC serial. She teaches part-time on the Sheffield Hallam Writing MA and has just completed a new novel, *Island*. She lives in Lancashire with Mike Harris and their two children.

Carol Shields was born and brought up in suburban Chicago, and has lived in Canada for more than three decades. Her novels include *Mary Swann* (1990), *Happenstance* (1991) and *The Republic of Love* (1992). *The Stone Diaries* was short-listed for the 1993 Booker Prize and *Larry's Party* won the 1998 Orange Prize for fiction. She has published one collection of short stories, *Various Miracles* (1994).

Ali Smith was born in Inverness, Scotland in 1962. Her book of short stories, *Free Love* (1995), won the Saltire First Book of the Year Award and a Scottish Arts Council Book Award. Her first novel, *Like* (1997), was nominated for the Saltire Award.

PERMISSIONS

The Women's Press would like to thank the following:

Bloomsbury Publishing Plc for permission to reprint 'Hack Wednesday' from *Wilderness Tips* by Margaret Atwood, 1991; and 'The Wedding Dress' from *The Blue Woman* by Mary Flanagan, 1994.

The Estate of Angela Carter, care of Rogers, Coleridge & White Ltd, 20 Powis Mews, London W11 1JN, for permission to reprint 'The Company of Wolves' from *The Bloody Chamber* by Angela Carter, 1979. Copyright © Angela Carter 1979.

Helen Dunmore, care of AP Watt, for permission to reprint 'Girls on Ice' from *Love of Fat Men*, 1997. Copyright © Helen Dunmore 1997.

Githa Hariharan, care of David Godwin, for permission to reprint 'Love Poem' from *The Art of Dying*, 1993.

Little, Brown for permission to reprint 'Fish' from *During Mother's Absence* by Michèle Roberts, 1994; and 'The World With Love' from *Free Love* by Ali Smith, 1998.

The Women's Press is Britain's leading women's publishing house. Established in 1978, we publish high-quality fiction and non-fiction from outstanding women writers worldwide. Our exciting and diverse list includes literary fiction, detective novels, biography and autobiography, health, women's studies, handbooks, literary criticism, psychology and self-help, the arts, our popular Livewire Books series for young women and the bestselling annual *Women Artists Diary* featuring beautiful colour and black-and-white illustrations from the best in contemporary women's art.

If you would like more information about our books or about our mail order book club, please send an A5 sae for our latest catalogue and complete list to:

The Sales Department
The Women's Press Ltd
34 Great Sutton Street
London EC1V 0DX
Tel: 0171 251 3007
Fax: 0171 608 1938